PUFFIN

THE LAST FIREFOX

Lee Newbery lives with his husband, son and two dogs in a seaside town in West Wales. By day, he helps vulnerable people look for jobs and gain new skills, and by night, he sits down at his laptop to write.

Lee enjoys adventuring, drinking ridiculous amounts of tea and giving his dogs a good cuddle – or a *cwtch*, as they say in Wales.

LEE NEWBERY

THE LAST FIREFOX

ILLUSTRATED BY **LAURA CATALÁN**

PUFFIN

PUFFIN BOOKS

UK | USA | Canada | Ireland | Australia
India | New Zealand | South Africa

Puffin Books is part of the Penguin Random House group of companies
whose addresses can be found at global.penguinrandomhouse.com.

www.penguin.co.uk
www.puffin.co.uk
www.ladybird.co.uk

First published 2022

005

Text copyright © Lee Newbery, 2022
Illustrations copyright © Laura Catalán, 2022

The moral right of the author and illustrator has been asserted

Text design by Ken de Silva
Printed in Great Britain by Clays Ltd, Elcograf S.p.A.

The authorized representative in the EEA is Penguin Random House Ireland,
Morrison Chambers, 32 Nassau Street, Dublin D02 YH68

A CIP catalogue record for this book is available from the British Library

ISBN: 978–0–241–49353–3

All correspondence to:
Puffin Books
Penguin Random House Children's
One Embassy Gardens, 8 Viaduct Gardens, London SW11 7BW

Penguin Random House is committed to a
sustainable future for our business, our readers
and our planet. This book is made from Forest
Stewardship Council® certified paper.

This, the book of my heart,

for Tom and Parker, the people of my soul

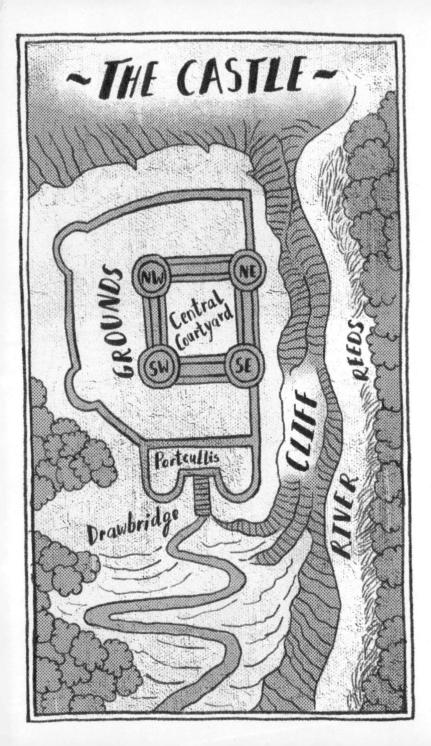

Chapter 1

I'm being chased to my death by a goose and it's all Lippy's fault.

If it wasn't for her and her crazy ideas, I wouldn't be in this mess. Take the pebble game, for example. She came up with it months ago, after reading about families hiding pebbles in parks for other families to find. First you paint a pebble and, when you find another one out in the world, you swap it for your own so someone else can find it, and so the game goes on. Well, Lippy decided we needed to do our own version.

And, when Lippy decides something, Roo and I have no choice but to play along. We take it in turns to hide a painted pebble somewhere around Bryncastell, where we live, and post a clue in our group chat. The first person who finds it keeps the pebble and gets to hide theirs next.

It was fun at first, but then Lippy's hiding places started getting more, well, let's just say *imaginative*. Only two weeks ago, Roo had to ask the man at the pet stall in the market to scoop Lippy's pebble out of one of the fish tanks. Before that, I had to rummage through a ball pit at the indoor play area in town, while little kids bounced on my head.

So, when Lippy sent her latest clue, Roo and I weren't exactly scrambling to get to the pebble first.

You will find it in the House of Ducks.

I don't know how she comes up with this stuff.

Roo took one look at me and shook his head. 'You can have this one.'

It took a lot of deciphering, but I finally decided

that the nesting box on the edge of the lake in the park was the only place in the whole of Bryncastell that Lippy could possibly mean by the 'House of Ducks'.

The nesting box is a small wooden hut built on a platform just a little way out on the lake. It's basically a mansion for ducks. All I had to do was hop on to the platform, lean through the tiny doorway and grab Lippy's pebble.

Sounds easy, eh?

And it was, to begin with. I made sure there were no ducks around and leaped on to the platform. Then I got down on all fours and poked my head through the doorway.

It was quite cosy inside, if a bit smelly. Lots of hay and other duck stuff. And there, nestled in the hay, was the pebble. It was perfectly circular and smooth, and painted on it was the sun, with warm yellow rays rippling outwards.

Aha!

My joy was short-lived. I was just reaching out to pick it up when I heard a nasty-sounding hiss from outside. My whole body tensed, and I slowly retreated out of the wooden box, bottom first.

Until today, I didn't really have much of an opinion on geese. I know swans can be vicious, with their twisty never-ending necks and wings that can break your arm with a single beat, but I've never really given geese a lot of thought.

Well, now I know the truth: geese are the most fearsome beasts to roam the Earth.

This particular goose was enormous. It was definitely the boss goose. It had beady black eyes, full of rage, and a mouth full of tiny serrated spikes for teeth.

It fixed me with its glare and very slowly, very menacingly, said, '*Honk.*'

I let out a whimper. I had to get out of there.

As though it had read my thoughts, the goose stretched up high and extended its wings. It started beating them powerfully and lunged at me. I screamed and dived for the muddy bank a metre or so away.

And missed.

Turns out that reversing out of a duck house butt first is a guaranteed way of messing with your senses. I completely misjudged where I was and leaped in the wrong direction. Instead of the ground, my feet found water and I went under.

The cold was a shock. I don't like the cold. I like pyjamas that have just come out of the tumble dryer and socks with a little bit of extra fluff.

Well, the lake had no extra fluff. It had extra gunk and slime and sludge, oh yes, but *zero* fluff.

I broke the surface, gasping for air, with a lily pad stuck to my face. Then something soft hit my cheek and bounced into the water, like somebody was throwing marshmallows at me. I peeled away the lily pad and stared at the bank of the lake.

An old lady was standing there, and next to her was Lucy, a girl I recognized from school. She has golden hair and a winning smile, but right then she was gawping at me.

And then something else hit my face.

'Er, Nan,' said Lucy. I saw recognition flicker across

her features, but there was something else, too. Pity, perhaps? 'That's not a duck. You can stop throwing bread.'

The old lady lowered the loaf of stale bread she'd been tearing chunks from (apparently having completely ignored the '**Do not feed bread to the ducks**' sign just off the bank). She peered at me over the rim of her glasses. 'It's not? I thought it looked a bit odd. What is it, then?'

'It's, er, a hairless dog, I think,' said Lucy. 'And it's about to get eaten by an angry goose, so let's go.' She shepherded her elderly grandmother away.

Well, that was humiliating. My cheeks burned so hot I swear the water started evaporating –

Wait. Did Lucy just say . . . ?

There was a triumphant hiss behind me. I glanced over my shoulder and let out another whimper. The goose glared at me, sunlight glinting off its needle teeth.

'*Honk*,' it said again, and then rocketed forward.

'Aaaaaaaaaaaaaargh!'

I didn't waste another second. I splashed to the shore and legged it, my pockets full of water and my shoes squelching fartily with every step.

Which brings me to now – running through the park with a goose chasing after me.

I think of my dads. I think of Lippy and Roo. I think of all the things I haven't had the chance to do yet, like have a bath in hot chocolate and hide in a comic-book shop until it closes so I can spend the night there.

This is rubbish. I'm going to be goose food.

And the worst part? I forgot to pick up that stupid pebble.

Chapter 2

It's all a bit of a blur, but in the end I manage to lose the goose by hurling myself into a hedge. I wriggle my way through, my clothes getting snagged on thorns. The monster snaps its jaws at me from the other side. I spare it a final glance before setting off for home, humiliated and defeated, my dignity left somewhere in the lake like a dead fish.

When I get back, I nip upstairs and change into some dry clothes. Dad is in the hallway when I come back down, standing on a stool and stretching up towards the ceiling with a screwdriver. His face lights up when he spots me.

'Charlie!' he booms. 'How was school? Hey, wanna see what I'm doing? I'm installing a brand-new, state-of-the-art smoke alarm. It's called the Heat Hunter Three Thousand, and it's got a special thermal detector –'

'That's really cool, Dad,' I call, 'but I gotta go. Er, I've got homework to do.'

I whizz into the kitchen and out of the back door before Dad can ask me why my hair is damp.

I cross the garden towards the great oak tree at the bottom. Nestled perfectly in the branches is a tree house. Dad built it a few years ago, and it's been my castle among the leaves ever since. It's got its own little veranda looking out over the garden, and a window.

I head for the dangling rope ladder and dart up the rungs into a world where nobody else exists. It's just me, a couple of beanbags and a box of supplies.

I've barely settled in with a comic book to calm me down after my near-death experience when I hear something below. A strangled squawk, like a bird with a cold. At first, I think the goose has found me, but then my shoulders relax. Of course it hasn't.

I cup my hands to my mouth and repeat the bird call back to whoever is below. Except I already know who it is. There are only two other people in the world who are in on our secret code.

The ladder creaks as somebody starts climbing. A second later, a head appears over the edge of the platform. It's a head that I would recognize anywhere. Thick black hair and caramel eyes. Rupert Baltazar.

Roo has been my best friend since nursery. His family is from the Philippines, although he's never actually been there himself. I glower at him as he hauls himself up on to the platform and into the tree house.

'You need to work on your bird call,' I tell him. 'It's croaky.'

Roo doesn't get a chance to answer because another call flutters up from the garden. This one is far more realistic.

'Lippy!' Roo yells. 'I've already done the call.

You don't need to do it as well!'

I squawk back down anyway, and immediately the ladder starts creaking again. Another head appears, this one belonging to a girl. She has a ton of curly red hair, a smattering of freckles and big green eyes. Philippa Tarquin, my second oldest best friend after Roo.

She glares at him. 'How do you know what's happened to me since you got up here? I could have been snatched away and somebody else might have taken my place.'

'You're in Charlie's garden, not the jungle, Lippy. It's not like you're gonna get abducted by an enemy tribe.'

Lippy clambers into the tree house. 'What's the point of having a secret signal if you're not going to use it? Hey, Charlie.'

'Hey.'

'Where did you disappear off to after school?'

My cheeks burn. 'Oh, I, er . . . went for a walk.'

Lippy narrows her eyes. 'Hmm, I smell porky-pies!'

'Me too,' Roo says, nodding.

'Oh, all right! If you *must* know, I went to look for your stupid pebble.'

Lippy's face lights up. 'And?'

'And I got chased by a goose, thanks to you! I didn't even have time to pick it up!'

Lippy and Roo glance at each other, and then they burst out laughing. Roo is actually rolling on the floor, wheezing. Lippy is slapping her knees.

'Oh, Charlie,' she gasps. 'At least you gave it a go.'

'I'm glad *you* went for this one,' says Roo.

I glare at them. 'It's not funny. That goose could have ripped me to shreds!'

I decide not to tell them about falling in the lake. I don't want to humiliate myself even further.

Lippy straightens up. 'You're right, Charlie. I'm sorry. I wouldn't have hidden the pebble there if I'd known there was a killer goose around. But, you know, you really should learn to stick up for yourself. If you can't stand up to a goose, how will –'

'Not this again,' I groan.

I get this talk from Lippy at least once a week. I've got a problem with bullying at school at the moment. Well, two problems. Their names are Will and Zack, and I'm their victim of choice.

They've been picking on me ever since we had our taster day at secondary school a few months ago. Lippy thinks it's because the idea of changing schools scares them, and they want to make themselves look less vulnerable by picking on the quietest person in class: me.

'It's not like *they're* that tough anyway,' Lippy once said. 'Will's mum phones to check up on him every lunch break, and Zack isn't allowed to go to the skate park unless he wears full-body padding. I mean elbow pads, knee pads, wrist guards *and* a helmet with smiley faces on it.'

Which, of course, makes me feel a million times worse about not being able to stand up to them.

'All right, all right,' says Lippy. 'Let's move on. I have *very* exciting news. You know how we break up for summer next week?'

I snort. It's like she thinks it hasn't occurred to me. But there's a bittersweet edge to this summer holiday: it's our last before secondary school. Year Seven is waiting for us, and it scares the daylights out of me.

I mean, I can't say I *love* Year Six. Obviously, I'd rather stay at home and read comics. But our teacher, Mrs Parry, is nice. She's a bit old-fashioned and sucks mints really loudly, but she's fine. I'm used to her. In secondary school, I'll have, like, twelve different teachers. How on earth am I supposed to get used to that many?

'And you know how on the second weekend of the summer holidays it's the Bryncastell Summer Fete?'

'Lippy, get on with it,' I say.

'And you know how my mum is on the planning committee for the Bryncastell Summer –'

'Lippy!'

'Fine!' Lippy huffs. 'Well, I've managed to get us a stall!'

A silence follows.

'A stall?' I finally say.

'Selling what?' asks Roo.

Lippy grins and delves into her bag. 'I've been working on a top-secret recipe.'

Oh no. I'm not sure I like the sound of this.

'Is this like the time you made banana pizza?' groans Roo.

'Not quite. No, this is something different. Something that will become a Bryncastell household brand.'

She pulls out her hands, holding a clear sandwich bag full of – well, it looks like green gunk.

'Ta-dah!'

There's an awkward silence.

'Um, a bag of bogeys?' I suggest.

'Ew, no! What I hold here is a test batch of *Philippa's Phat Hamster Salad*, Bryncastell's next top small-rodent food!'

Roo and I stare at her.

'It's happened,' he says to me.

'Yep,' I agree. 'She's completely lost the plot.'

'Oh, be quiet! I came up with it as a way of making

extra pocket money by selling it at my mum's surgery. All those little hamsters and mice and gerbils need something tasty, don't you think?'

Lippy's mother is a vet, and she runs her own practice in the middle of town, called Pet Hospital.

'OK, but what's in it?' I ask.

'Only the finest locally sourced ingredients. Mashed-up bran flakes, a dash of honey and green food colouring to make it look extra healthy. All from the Co-op down the road. I've tried it on my little sister's hamster, Dorito, and he loves it. Listen, are you going to help me with the stall or not?'

Roo and I exchange glances. We know there's no way we're going to be able to get out of this. This is what Lippy does. She comes up with these wild ideas, and then we have to go along with them.

'What's in it for us?' asks Roo.

'A lifetime supply of *Philippa's Phat Hamster Salad* for any small rodents that enter your care,' says Lippy, then sighs when she sees the expressions on our faces. 'Fine, you can each have twenty-five per cent of the profits.'

'Deal,' Roo and I say.

'Excellent. Roo, you can be in charge of the money. Charlie, you can handle the stock.'

'And what will *you* be doing?' I ask.

'I'll be getting us customers,' says Lippy, and she starts packing away the bag of green mush.

A voice flutters through the tree-house window from the house. 'Charlie, tea's ready!'

'I'd best get going, too,' Lippy declares. 'I need to make another practice batch. My sister said that Dorito's droppings came out a bit green, so I think I need to add less food colouring. Oh, and Charlie, I think it's only fair that you hide the next pebble. You did find the last one, after all. It's not your fault a goose chased you off before you could grab it. See you!'

She makes her way to the ladder and drops out of sight. Once she's gone, Roo turns to me.

'You realize what this means, don't you?' he says.

'What?'

'I don't know if you've noticed, but Lippy's hiding places are getting more and more extreme . . .'

'I nearly lost my life to a goose earlier so, yes, I have noticed.'

'Right. In that case, we need to end this game once and for all. You've got to hide the pebble somewhere that we'll *never* find it.'

I frown. 'But *where?*'

Roo shrugs. 'Up to you, my friend. Just make sure it's impossible. Right, I gotta go. See you tomorrow.'

'See you.' Roo shuffles over the edge of the platform and down the ladder.

I'm going to have to rack my brains for the perfect hiding place. But first it's time to have dinner with my family.

Chapter 3

'What're you thinking, Charlie?'

We're sitting round the dining table, tucking into platefuls of spaghetti bolognese.

I'm twirling my fork into a tangle of pasta, but not actually eating it. 'Just about where to hide my next pebble.'

'Oh, are you three still playing that game?' asks Pa, pushing his glasses up his nose.

'Yep, and it's my turn,' I say. 'Lippy hid hers in a

really good place, so I need somewhere better.'

'Where did she hide it?' asks Dad.

'Uh, near the lake.'

I'm not mentioning the incident with the crazy goose. It was bad enough telling Lippy and Roo. And I *definitely* don't want to tell them about me falling in the water.

'You'll think of somewhere,' says Dad through a mouthful of pasta.

Pa glances at him, his gaze full of unreadable words, and Dad pauses.

It's like they've got this weird way of talking to each other using only their minds. Sometimes I think they have whole unspoken conversations when I'm around.

'Hey, wanna hear about the new Heat Hunter Three Thousand?' Dad starts. 'It can sense heat, not just smoke but *heat*, and it's got customizable alarms and . . .'

Dad's a firefighter and he's got a real obsession with alarms, so once he gets going it's hard to make him stop. There's a fire extinguisher in every room in our house – even my tree house.

Everybody at school thinks my dad is really cool. He came in once with a few other firefighters to give a talk on fire safety, and they told this story about how Dad once rescued a little boy and his cat from a burning building. Afterwards, everybody just looked at me in a confused sort of way, as if they were wondering how somebody like *me* could be the kid of somebody like *him*.

Pa clears his throat, and Dad stops short.

'OK, erm, right, there's something we want to talk to you about,' says Dad, apparently following Pa's silent instructions. 'The thing is, Charlie, your pa and I have been talking a lot lately about the possibility of . . . well –'

When Dad appears unable to finish what he wants to say, Pa intervenes.

'Charlie, we're thinking of adopting another child. We want you to have a little brother or sister.'

I almost fall off my chair. Of everything they could

have said, that was the *last* thing I expected.

'*What?*'

'You must understand that we're not doing this because you're not enough,' Pa blurts out. 'We love you more than the whole world –'

'Yeah, I remember your birthday more often than I remember Pa's,' Dad interrupts.

'*All right,*' Pa says, scowling. 'It's just that we'd love our family to grow. We think we're ready for it. What do you think?'

My mouth drops open.

'Charlie?' Dad prompts. 'Please say something.'

They're waiting for my reaction, so I say the first thing that pops into my head. Except two things pop in at the same time, and they sort of crash together.

'Grawesome!'

Dad pulls a face. 'Er, what?'

'I mean great,' I say, and then I shake my head. 'I mean awesome. I mean grawesome?'

'Does that mean you're on board?' asks Pa. 'Because we're a unit, you know. How you feel about this is very important to us.'

'Of course I'm on board!' I exclaim. 'So, I'm going to have a little sister or brother?'

And, just like that, as I say the words out loud, panic washes over me. I feel my smile start to fade.

Pa rests his hand on top of Dad's. It makes my heart hurt because I should be happy – but suddenly all I feel is a roiling unease in the pit of my stomach.

'Yep,' says Dad, and Pa's eyes glisten. 'A little sister or brother.'

I paste on a grin, like it's the best news ever – and I know it should be, but it doesn't feel that way. And not because I'm worried Dad and Pa are bored of me. It's not even because I'm jealous that a little baby will get more attention.

Believe it or not, I'd *love* to have a little brother or sister. Dad and Pa know this – they've brought up adopting another child several times before, and I always thought I loved the idea. But now that they're actually talking about it seriously, well . . .

It's just that I know I won't be able to protect them. I'm not as brave as I'd like to be. And, when people like Will and Zack exist, you need to be brave. You need to be brave for yourself before you can be brave for other people.

But I'm not like my dad. I can't run into a burning building. I ran *away* from a goose. Dad always tells me I need to find my inner fire – well, what little inner fire I had was snuffed out as soon as I landed in that lake.

But I force another smile. 'That's brilliant news. I can't wait.'

My parents beam at each other. They start talking about their plans to convert the spare room into a nursery and how a social worker is supposed to be visiting us tomorrow for a quick chat.

My food remains untouched. Thankfully, Dad and Pa don't seem to notice. They're laughing together and they look so happy that my heart aches. Here we are, the Challinors. A family of three that's about to become four. I should be happy – except all I can think about is where I can get a big dose of bravery from as soon as possible.

Chapter 4

I wake up to a bank of storm clouds over Bryncastell, and by second lesson there are big fat drops falling from the sky.

My gaze wanders out of the window during Welsh – we're revising the names of different animals, like cat, dog, fish, fox – and finds the crooked grey structure of the castle on top of the hill at the edge of town. It sits sentry over the rooftops, guarding the houses and buildings that sprawl underneath. It's made up of four central towers, one of them leaning into the wind, and outer walls that have crumbled away in places, yet which are almost perfectly preserved in others. It's full of echoing chambers and twisting passages.

Just make sure we can't find it, Roo said.

That's it. That's the ideal place to hide the pebble!

Last lesson is art. Because it's the end of term, Mrs Parry lets us make anything we want. I'm working on a family portrait made entirely out of dots, using the end of a brush dipped in paint. I'm not the best artist in Year Six, but I'm proud of what I've done. My ears are a bit big, and Pa's jaw is a bit wonky, but I think I've captured the essence of us. The happiness.

I'm imagining a fourth face in the picture, a younger sister or brother cuddling up to us, when I hear a sound in my left ear.

'*Hiiiiiiiiissssssssssssssssssss* . . .'

I flinch and whirl round — and find myself looking up at an unpleasantly familiar face. My heart sinks.

'So the rumours are true,' Will sniggers. 'You

really are scared of geese! You're even more pathetic than I thought.'

The blood rushes to my cheeks. How does he know? And then I remember – Lucy saw me. I look over my shoulder. She's sitting a few tables away, chatting to her friends. My cheeks may never go back to their normal colour, thanks to her.

'Whatcha drawing there, goose food?' asks Will.

He has a mop of blond hair and is shorter than me

by about half a head. He's not really much of a threat when he's on his own, but when he's with his crony he takes on the attitude of a yappy little Jack Russell terrier. Zack stands behind him now, a bespectacled giant. He doesn't say much, but he's always there, being ridiculously tall and sniggering at Will's jokes.

I don't answer. Will peers down at my portrait and smirks.

'What a pretty picture!' he coos. 'But wait, I'm confused . . . who's that little girl in the middle?'

Zack makes a series of grunting noises that I think is laughter.

'Get lost, Will,' says Lippy.

Will grimaces at her, as though he's only just realized she's there. They don't pick on me when Lippy is around, mainly because she comes up with all these ludicrous threats that they're never quite sure she'll carry out or not.

'You can't talk to me like that,' he scoffs.

'And *you* can't comment on somebody's artwork when you haven't even learned how to colour inside the lines yet,' says Lippy. 'Now get lost, or I'll give you a paper cut between your toes.'

I don't know how she comes up with this stuff. But also – *ouch*.

Will fumbles for a response, but then Roo starts making a weird growling noise. Zack shuffles uncomfortably behind his leader.

'What's he doing?' he mutters, and then Roo barks. Like an *actual* bark.

Will shakes his head. 'Come on, let's leave these freaks to it.'

They disappear, and Lippy and Roo get back to work.

I stare at them. 'What on earth was that?'

'What?' asks Lippy, picking up her brush.

'You, with the paper cuts? And Roo, with the barking!'

'Oh, that was just an empty threat,' says Lippy. 'I'd never actually go near their feet. Ew.'

'And I decided to weird them out,' says Roo. 'Sometimes you just have to do something so unexpected they have no idea how to react and then they leave you alone.'

Lippy nods. 'You just need to figure out what works for you. They'll soon leave you alone if you learn how to stand up to them.'

I'm left staring at my portrait. A boy with mousy brown hair and misty blue eyes. I want him to be the sort of boy who can fend for himself, not rely on his friends to do it for him. I need some of their fire if I'm ever going to be a good big brother.

I just don't know where I can get it from.

By the time school ends, the rain has slowed to a drizzle, and I decide to go up to the castle to hide my pebble. On it I've painted what's supposed to be a blossoming fire, but which really just looks like a splodge of orange, yellow and red paint. I've got my portrait with me, too. Since it's the end of the year, we get to take our work home with us. Mrs Parry let me borrow a plastic portfolio case to keep it dry.

I'm just heading on to the hedgerow path when they get me. My hood is pulled up against the rain, and I don't see them coming until it's too late.

A shove from behind and the next thing I know I'm sprawled on the ground. Mud splashes into my eyes and mouth. Rainwater seeps through my clothes, chills my skin.

I cough and splutter. Something is ripped from my fingers. Through the mud that clogs my eyes I see them: Will and Zack are standing over me, their hoods up. They seem less interested in me and more interested in what Zack holds – my art portfolio.

'Open it,' Will commands, a nasty grin on his face, and Zack obeys.

'No!' I shout, scrambling to my knees, but Will shoves me back down.

'Do it!' he yells. 'Not brave enough to face us on your own, goose food?'

I know what Lippy would say if she was here. *Not brave enough to ambush me on your own, Will?*

But I can't say it. Even though it's true. I can only

watch in horror as Zack tilts the portfolio upside down. Out slips my family portrait, fluttering into the open like a butterfly being released. But then the rain hits it and it drops to the earth. It lands face up. I can see our smiling faces.

I try to rescue it, but Will pins me to the ground. Then Zack steps forward and grinds my portrait into the mud with his foot. I'm too numb to move, helpless as he mashes my painting into the sodden earth.

By the time he's done, I can't tell what's mud and what's portrait.

'Come on, let's go to the skate park,' says Will, jabbing his accomplice in the shoulder. They spare me one last glance before bolting away, leaving me alone in the mud.

I haul myself to my knees and rake my fingers through the muck. I grab at soggy scraps of paper, but most of it disintegrates in my hands.

I feel hopeless. It wasn't the best portrait in the world, but it was *my* portrait. *My* family. And now it's gone. And I let it happen.

I'm not quite sure how long I sit there in the dirt before I start moving again. The rain stops and the clouds begin to part, but I'm still drenched as I make my way along the path. The castle looms overhead, its walls dark with rain.

I still need to hide my pebble. I wonder if maybe I can hide my fear as well.

After about five minutes of walking, I decide that I don't really like castles. They're always on top of these ginormous hills. My legs feel as though they're about to drop off.

The castle inches closer until finally the ground starts to level off. It sits atop the hill like a sleeping giant, watching the seasons roll by. From up here, I can see for miles around – the endless fields, the dark blue shadows of mountains in the distance and Bryncastell just below.

I reach into my school bag, my hand closing round the pebble. I need to hide it somewhere Lippy and Roo will *never* find it, so this ridiculous game can end.

As I make my way over the drawbridge and under the portcullis, I feel as though I've stepped into the past, to a time where there's no Will and Zack, no concerns over being a good older brother. I spot the tourist information board with the map that I used to love looking at when I was younger. It shows the open grounds inside the castle, which surround four towers. The towers are connected by four walls, enclosing the central courtyard at the very heart of the ruins. I study it, wondering where the best place to hide the pebble would be.

According to the information board, the north-west tower is the best preserved. It's the only one that members of the public are allowed to climb. I glance up and see the four inner towers stretching to the sky. The others are either a bit wonky or have crumbled over the years. The north-west tower, however, still stands proud.

Perfect.

I make my way round the grounds that encircle the towers, heading for the archway in the wall at the bottom of the north-west tower, which leads to a staircase. It's all the way over on the other side of the castle, and I pass huge piles of rubble and a  crumbling stone furnace on my way.

I peer through the archway and find myself gazing up the spiral staircase that disappears into the darkness of the north-west tower. I've never been up there before; it always looked a bit *too* creepy. I cast a quick glance over my shoulder before dipping through.

The stairs seem to go on forever, but finally I emerge on to a circular roof, fenced in with battlements. The world falls away from me. Bryncastell clusters below me to one side, a little toy village, with a rushing river and the wilderness

beyond on the other.

I walk to the edge and find a small pile of rubble where part of the turret has crumbled away. Heaving some of the bigger stones aside, I tuck the pebble into a crevice and cover it up. I picture Lippy and Roo's faces when I send my clue to our group chat.

You'll find it at the highest spot in town.

Hmm, no. That's too easy.

To find the next pebble, you need to head north-west.

That will do. It sounds vague, but the location is actually in the clue: the north-west tower. *Still, they'll never find it*, I think triumphantly. Roo will be pleased.

I head back down to the grounds, feeling proud of my cleverness. I emerge through the archway at the bottom of the tower and pause to look around. I'm standing in the walled-in clearing that forms the top-right corner of the castle's map. The far wall is hidden by a curtain of ivy. It looks perfectly ordinary, but there's a distant sound coming from behind it.

I tilt my head. No, surely it can't be. There's nothing but ancient, solid stone behind that ivy. I take a few steps closer, until the veil of dark emerald leaves is only a metre away.

But there it is again, whispering through the leaves. Getting louder and louder until it sounds like footsteps. The footsteps of somebody coming towards me. Somebody in a hurry.

'Aaaaaaaaaaaaaargh!'

And, before I can get out of the way, that somebody comes bursting through the ivy and knocks right into me, sending me flying through the air.

Chapter 5

For a second, I think I must have bumped my head because when I look up from the ground there's a boy standing over me, dressed in these weird clothes. Weirder still, he's carrying an orange puppy.

Definitely must have bumped my head. I try to blink him away, but he doesn't fade. Then he starts talking and I start to suspect he's not a side effect of my bumped head after all.

He's wearing a brown fur coat that rises and falls rapidly on his shoulders as he pants. He's been running. He keeps glancing over his shoulder towards the ivy, as if he's worried about being followed.

'Erm. Who are you?' I ask, clambering to my feet.

'Nobody,' he insists. He glances at the puppy in his arms, then looks me up and down. 'Hmm. You're a bit small, but you'll have to do. Here, hold him.'

And, just like that, I have a puppy in my arms. It's a chubby little thing, all big ears and cheese-puff-orange fur, which is strangely warm. It's like hugging a hot-water bottle. And that's when I realize – this puppy has a long, bushy tail and too-pointy ears. In fact, there's something decidedly *un*puppyish about it . . .

'It's a fox!' I exclaim, holding it back out to Nobody. The cub dangles between us and lets out a little whine. 'Hey, I don't want it!'

Nobody stands up straight, his expression severe. 'It's a *he*. His name is Firetail. And don't hold him like that. Keep him close to you.'

I stare dumbly down at the cub before clutching him to my chest so that his heart beats rapidly against mine. 'Why is he called Firetail –'

I'm cut off by a piercing howl. It turns the air cold and makes the hairs on the back of my neck stand on end – and it's coming from behind the ivy. Now that I'm looking closely, I can see fragments of darkness through the greenery.

There's no wall there at all. It's a *doorway*.

The stranger's eyes widen in fear. 'You're about to find out. Put him down. Hurry!'

I frown and lower the cub to the ground, and through the ivy the howling stops abruptly. The cub's hackles rise, a growl rumbling in his belly. Then, unbelievably, his fur starts shimmering. He glows brighter and brighter, and I feel a prickle of heat on my skin. It's almost like he's on –

'Get back!' the boy shouts, shielding his face – but it's too late. The cub erupts on the spot, an orb of angry fire bursting from his body. I leap back, the flames so bright that I can barely look at them.

After a few seconds, I peer through my fingers. The flames have mostly died down, and there's the

cub, still standing in a ball of orange fire, completely unscathed and snarling at the ivy.

I can't believe what I'm seeing. Maybe I *did* bump my head.

'That happens when he's angry or scared or excited,' the boy says hurriedly. 'And sometimes when he's hungry. Now I really have to go. I'll be back to pick him up in two days –'

'*What?*' I exclaim. 'You can't leave him here with me! What is he? Who are you? And *what on earth* is going on here?'

The boy peers through the ivy, then back at me, his eyes wide with fear. 'There's no time to explain. The Grendilock is hot on my trail, and I really have to lead it away or it'll follow me through and we'll all be done for.'

'The *what?*'

The boy groans. 'Through there,' he says, pointing over his shoulder at the ivy, 'is a place called Fargone. A fantastical place where the giant emperor rats can eat you for breakfast, and the sky-whales roost in the

clouds. I got here using this –'
He pulls out an amber stone
with a swirl painted on it. 'It's
a sealstone. This one belongs
to the king – or at least it did
before I took it. But we don't want
him to find out about this gateway because he's the
one who's after *him*.'

He nods his head at the cub. The little fox has
crawled between his legs and is nervously peering
round them. His fur still looks fiery, but it's calmed
down a lot.

'W-why?'

The boy's expression darkens. 'Firefoxes have been
kept by the Royal Family in Fargone for centuries,
but through neglect and carelessness they started
to die out. The royals are selfish: all they want is to
showcase their pets. I witnessed Firetail's own mother
dying within those cold castle walls. It's no life for a
firefox. They need to be free. A firefox hasn't been
seen in the wild for over a hundred years. For all we

know, Firetail here is the last one – and so I vowed to find him a new home.'

'You mean you stole him?'

'Well, you could put it like that. I think of it more as rescuing him.'

'C-can't you just keep him?'

The cub eyes me dubiously before looking up at his rescuer. He's clearly saying, *You can't leave me here with him. Look at him! He wouldn't say boo to a goose.*

Well, he's got a point. The last goose I bumped into said boo to me.

'Dastardly dragons, no!' the boy exclaims. 'I work in the royal kitchens. I haven't got time to look after a firefox. I'm just his guardian until I find him a better home.'

'And what makes you think I can give him a better home?'

He frowns. 'Absolutely nothing. What gave you that idea? If anything, you've got a bit of a frightened look about you. But you'll have to do. It's only for a day or two while I lead the Grendilock away.'

There's that word again. 'The Grendilock?'

Before he can reply, another howl slithers through the ivy. It's closer this time, running up my spine like an icy fingernail.

'*That's* the Grendilock,' he whispers. 'Accomplice to the king, and seeking His Majesty's only remaining firecub. The Royal Guard noticed his absence from the menagerie, and, ever since, the king has been in a royal rage. He ordered a reward for the return of Firetail. The Grendilock is a terrible thing. It can take many forms, its favourite being the hound. But they're all monstrous in their own way – and, right now, it's close!'

The next sound that thunders through the ivy is a bark. A furious, rumbling bark that rattles my ribcage. Firetail lets out a squeaky cry.

'I have to go,' says the boy, picking up the fox and plopping him in my arms again. 'Here, take him. You need to get used to each other.'

Firetail looks up at me mistrustfully, and, just when it looks like he's about to leap away from me, the howl returns. It's even louder, like the wailing wind on a stormy night.

Instantly, the cub changes his mind about trying to escape and burrows deeper into my chest. I feel a warmth spread down my front, and my heart pounds as I recognize what's about to happen.

He's heating up. He's going to burst into flames – in my arms!

But then the warmth starts to *smell*, and I let out a horrified gasp as I realize what's really happened.

'He's peed on me!' I cry, plonking the cub on the ground. He darts over to his guardian and cowers between his legs again.

'Oh, that's brilliant!' the boy says delightedly.

I gawp at him. 'Eh?'

'Pass me your jacket. I can use it to lead the Grendilock away. It's got an excellent sense of smell.'

I do as I'm told, wriggling out of my jacket and tossing it to him. He bundles it into a ball, then eyes me imploringly. 'You must look after him. I'll meet you back here in two days, at midday. Until then, keep him safe.'

He leans down, scoops up the cub and holds him out to me.

I take the little animal uncertainly. He feels soft and podgy in my arms, and his fur looks like ordinary fox fur again.

'Here, before I forget, take this,' says the stranger, digging into his pockets. He presses something into my palm. It's a metallic disc, a bit like a watch face, set with delicate cogs that glint in the sun.

'What is it?' I frown.

'It's how you're going to contact me if anything goes wrong, which it *won't*.' He pulls out an identical gizmo. 'I have its brother. If you turn the cogs on yours, it will activate the cogs on mine and I'll know to come and find you. It acts as a sort of compass, too. It will lead me to you, wherever you are. It's called a pennycog. Give it a go.'

I use my finger to wind the little cogs on my disc.

When I let go, the cogs begin to spin – and, to my amazement, so do the cogs on his. One of the dials has an arrow engraved on it, which whirls round until it finally settles and points directly at me.

'Good,' he says, nodding. 'Now I really have to go. I've wasted enough time already.'

He turns to make his exit, and I feel a rush of panic.

'Wait!' I shout. 'Who are you?'

The boy hesitates. 'Teg,' he finally says. 'And you?'

'Charlie.'

Teg flashes me a quick smile. 'Charlie, as soon as I've stepped through the gateway, run. I'm going to close it as quick as I can. Got it?'

I nod, my heart pounding. With that, Teg pushes through the ivy and vanishes from sight. The howl immediately comes again, louder than before.

I don't waste any time. I bolt round the corner with the cub tucked into my chest and press myself against the wall. After a few seconds, I peer back into the clearing.

At first, I can still hear the shrieking howl – but then, suddenly, it stops. A breeze rustles the ivy and, instead of blackness behind the leaves, I see the familiar cold stone of the castle walls.

The gateway is closed. Teg must have used the sealstone, and now he's making a run for it. I don't know who he is, or even if all of this is real, but I hope he gets away. I wouldn't want to meet whatever's making that dreadful howling face-to-face.

I look down and see the cub's huge amber eyes blinking up at me from my arms.

What have I got myself into?

Chapter 6

Ten minutes ago, I was on my way up to the castle to hide my pebble. Now I'm on my way down from the castle, and I *did* hide my pebble, but I have also acquired a highly flammable fox cub.

Ugh. Why do all these things happen to me? First the goose, now this.

So I'm heading down the hill with a firecub cradled in my arms. My empty art portfolio swings from my hand, caked with mud. Firetail stares up at me.

'You don't *look* like a Firetail,' I say.

He stares up at me like I'm stupid.

Of course I look like a Firetail, I can almost hear him saying. *Did you see me back there?*

'Hmm, no. That name doesn't fit. I'm gonna think of something else.'

What am I going to do with him? I can't take him into the house – what if he sets fire to something? There's always the tree house, which Dad has fully flameproofed using a special chemical spray. And he can't escape because he won't be able to get down the rope ladder.

At least there's no school tomorrow. Now *that* would be interesting. And he'll be gone by Sunday night. *It's just two days*, I tell myself. *Two days, and then everything will go back to normal.*

'At least you're cute,' I say. 'It could be worse. You could be a firespider, or a fiery naked mole rat.'

Firetail blinks at me. He looks as unsure of me as I feel about him.

I don't make eye contact with anybody as I trek

through town, which isn't unusual for me. I'm a head-down-walk-fast kinda guy. But today I'm walking extra fast, and my head is extra down, as I don't want to draw any attention to myself.

Which is hard when you're cradling a fox cub against your chest.

'Aw, what a cute puppy!' a passing girl squeals to her father, and I relax slightly. I'm glad it's not just me who's made that mistake when his flames aren't showing.

I'm approaching our house when Firetail starts wriggling in my arms. He lets out an irritated whine.

'What's wrong?' I ask, and suddenly his coat begins to heat up under my fingertips. 'OK, OK!'

I glance up and down the street to make sure there's nobody around before putting him down. Instantly, his fur begins to dim.

'Rude,' I mutter. 'All that fuss just to get your own way. What's wrong anyway? Ah, I see . . .'

I watch as he waddles over to an unfamiliar car that's parked directly outside our house, cocks his leg and begins to wee on one of the wheels.

The front door of my house opens. I freeze as the cub keeps weeing. I was going to go straight through to the back garden. I didn't want to get caught by my parents and have to explain to them –

But it's not my parents standing in the doorway. It's a woman with brown hair and a kind face, a colourful bag swinging from her shoulder. My dads appear behind her as she makes her way down the garden with a wave. She pauses when she spots me.

'Oh, you must be Charlie!' she says, beaming.

I'm rooted to the spot. Firetail has finally lowered his leg.

Please stay still, I urge silently. Where he's standing, the wheel is blocking him from sight.

'Er, yes, that's me,' I say, trying my best to sound normal.

'Fabulous!' says the woman. 'My name's Pam – I'm an adoption social worker. I just popped in to talk to your dads.'

Of course – with everything that's happened

today, I'd completely forgotten about the visit from a social worker. And Firetail just peed on her car!

'Oh!' I exclaim. 'Nice to meet you.'

'You too. I was just explaining to your dads that the adoption process should be plain sailing as they've already been through it once,' Pam trills. 'Are you looking forward to having a little brother or sister?'

I plaster on a smile. Not only is Firetail sniffing nervously round my feet, but now I also have to pretend I *am* excited. 'Oh yeah. I, er, really can't wait.'

'Wonderful! I'll be calling back soon. Maybe we can have a bit more of a chat then?'

'Erm, yeah, that would be nice.'

She slips through the gate and on to the pavement. She's getting close. I quickly lean down, scoop Firetail up and pull my school bag round to my front to cover him. As Pam climbs into her car, I scamper down the path and wave at my dads, slipping through to the back garden before they can call me over. I don't want to pause to talk – what would I say?

Sorry I'm late – I was just talking to a stranger from a

magical kingdom who gave me this living bonfire to look after for a few days. What's for dinner?

They'd freak. Especially Dad – it's literally his job to put out fires. What would he do if he saw Firetail? I'm just going to have to be really weird and evade any human contact whatsoever for the next two days.

Shouldn't be too difficult. Weird is my default setting. *Except*, I think, as I slip through the garden fence and make my way towards the tree house, *what about Lippy and Roo? How am I going to keep Firetail a secret from them?*

I hoist myself over the platform and into the tree house, sending Firetail spilling on to the boards. He freezes, taking in this brand-new setting, and then starts patrolling the perimeter of the room, his nose pressed to the floor.

I'm going to spend the whole weekend in the tree house, tucked away from the world, I decide. If I can just keep him calm and happy, then there'll be nothing to worry about. What was it Teg said about his fire? It flares up when he's angry or scared or excited, and sometimes when he's hungry, so I just need to make sure he's none of those things.

Should be easy, right?

It's not the best plan. Not a *fireproof* plan. But, as Firetail pounces on my beanbag and begins to savage it, it's the only one I've got.

'Oh, I don't know, Charlie. Isn't it a bit chilly for that?' says Pa.

We're in the kitchen. I've just asked my dads if I can sleep in the tree house tonight. It's something I do regularly in the summer.

'You know it's July, right?' Dad says to Pa. 'It's beautiful out there, and we're not forecast any hurricanes tonight.'

Pa huffs and waves a ladle at Dad. 'Fine! But if a storm hits I'm blaming you.'

My body hums with adrenaline. I left Firetail up in the tree house, sleeping soundly after an hour of wrestling a beanbag, which ended up singed when he got a bit overexcited and his flames came out. Once he'd established that the tree house was safe, he shed his anxiety and started running around like a maniac.

I change into pyjama bottoms and a hoodie, then grab my sleeping bag, a pillow and an old stuffed toy frog before heading back down to the kitchen. I pinch some corned beef and a few other treats, as well as a bottle of water and a bowl.

I open the back door and step out into the twilight. To my relief, the tree house is still standing –

I half expected to find it engulfed in flames, like an enormous blazing broccoli.

I carry my supplies up the ladder and find Firetail still snoozing against a beanbag. He snaps to attention as I enter, then relaxes when he sees me. I set everything down and sit opposite him.

'Don't worry, it's only me,' I say. 'You're a bit nervy, too, eh? I can relate.'

I peel open a pack of corned beef. Instantly, Firetail's nose wiggles.

'I thought that would work.'

I offer the slice of meat. He picks his way towards me, his nostrils flaring.

'I'm not going to hurt you. I'm here to look after you.'

He sniffs at my offering, then snatches it out of my hand with such speed that it startles me. I can feel the pleasant warmth from his fur as he chomps, his entire body taking on a gently shimmering quality. The sky outside is darkening, but he's providing all the light I need. I feel like I'm in a volcanic grotto.

'You need a new name,' I say. 'I still don't think Firetail is right. How about . . . Rocket?'

He shoots me a withering glance.

'No? OK . . . how about Dave?'

He doesn't even grace this suggestion with a response. I can't say I blame him.

I come up with name after name, but none of them seem to fit. I go from the obvious, like Ember and Comet, to names inspired by appearance, like Bushy and Rusty. They just don't feel right. But then I cast my mind back to our Welsh lesson, to the animal names that we learned today. The Welsh word for fox . . .

'Cadno,' I say.

The cub looks up, his ears twitching. It's like that was already his name and somebody just said it aloud for the first time.

'Ah, so *that's* what it is,' I grin. 'Cadno. I like it.'

I feed him the rest of the beef before

settling down against the beanbag. Cadno carries the stuffed frog over and urges me into a tug of war. I laugh as he yanks, putting his entire chubby body into the game.

Maybe this won't be so bad, I think to myself as I toy with the pennycog in my pocket. Teg said to use it if I ran into any bother – that it would alert his own pennycog, and he'd know to come and find us. But Cadno doesn't seem to be any trouble – and he *is* extremely cute.

Here, with the cub yanking at my toy frog, a playful little growl rumbling in his chest like laughter, I feel a million impossible things become real. Maybe I won't need to use the pennycog at all.

'Nice to meet you, Cadno,' I say.

My dreams are filled with howling. A wolf wail that echoes through the night. The Grendilock continues its hunt, getting closer and closer with every sniff . . .

I open my eyes. The night is still. Cadno is curled up against me, his paws digging into my side, and everything is as it should be.

Except I'm sure I can hear a *real* howl, way off in the distance, creeping down from the hills. Maybe it's just the residue of my dream, but, as the moon reaches its highest point in the sky, I gather up a snoring Cadno and head inside, up to my bedroom.

Just in case.

Chapter 7

I'm woken by a wet, scratchy sensation on my cheek. I open my eyes to see a glistening black nose looming just centimetres from my face. Behind it is a pair of amber eyes and, thankfully, a face full of normal fox fur. Not a flame in sight.

'G'morning,' I mutter.

Cadno's tongue lolls from his mouth. He looks like he's waiting for something . . .

'Do you need the loo? Is that what it is?' I sit up,

pale morning light filtering
through the windows. 'Come on,
then. It's time for you to do your business.'

I scoop him up and carefully creep on to the
landing. It's still very early – I can hear Dad snoring in
his and Pa's bedroom.

Once I'm outside, I set Cadno down, his padded
paws sinking into the grass. He's got the singed
remains of the stuffed frog dangling from his mouth
and is surveying his surroundings mistrustfully.

'Don't worry, it's only the garden – nothing here to hurt you,' I say.

I don't look as he goes about his private business. I wouldn't want anybody watching me, so I turn round just as he starts to do a number two. But then I hear a sharp sound and feel a burst of heat against my back.

I almost don't want to look. I just want to keep staring at the flower beds and pretend that there isn't a firefox up to mischief behind me. But that would be irresponsible, so I turn – and let out a huge gasp.

Cadno has leaped up at the clothes line and is now suspended in mid-air, his jaws clamped round a sock – his whole body a bright, blazing ball of fire. He's wriggling so wildly that the entire line is starting to flap. Fire climbs up the sock and travels along the clothes line, to a towel, to a pillowcase, so that within seconds it's turned into a fiery storm in the middle of our garden.

I can do nothing but gawp.

Cadno growls playfully, and then the sock that he's swinging from disintegrates. He falls to the ground and starts zipping round the clothes line, leaping into the air as he tries to catch something else.

'Charlie, what's –' comes a voice from above. 'WHOA!'

I look up, and to my horror see Dad opening his bedroom window. His expression goes from sleepy-eyed to panic-stricken in an instant, and the next thing I know he's vanished from sight.

'No!' I hiss. '*Nonononono!*'

I whirl round and find Cadno proudly watching the fiery vortex he's created.

'Oi, you! Get away from there! Now!'

His ears droop when he realizes he's in trouble, his flames retreating. I lean over and find that his fur has cooled enough for me to grab him. I carry him up the tree-house ladder, nudge him inside and point a finger at him.

'Not a peep, OK?' I grumble. 'I'm gonna be in so much trouble because of you! He'd better not have seen you, otherwise I'm leaving you to do all the explaining. OK?'

Cadno hangs his head and looks away in embarrassment. I feel a twinge of guilt, but I don't have time to stick around. I hop back down to the ground just as Dad bursts through the back door. He's dressed only in his boxers, but, of course, he's carrying a fire extinguisher. He lets rip at the raging clothes line, a cloud of white spray bursting out. He aims it at the flames and sends smoke hissing into the air.

He doesn't look at all scared. He looks calm and focused, as if this is completely natural. Meanwhile, my heart feels like it's trying to hammer its way out of my ribcage. How can he confront a fire like that without even batting an eyelid?

It doesn't take long to douse the flames. By the time he's done, there are only a few blackened tatters left.

Dad turns off the extinguisher. Pa has appeared at the back door, his face white.

'What just happened?' Dad asks after what feels like an age.

Oh no. I was too busy watching him to come up with a believable excuse.

'Uh . . . well . . . I don't know,' I mumble. 'I was asleep in the tree house and the smoke woke me up. I don't know how it started.'

I decide to keep the truth about me moving inside during the night to myself. I hate lying to them, but I need my story to hang together.

'Are you sure?' Dad frowns. 'I could have sworn I saw a . . .'

'What?' asks Pa.

I feel like I might throw up, but then Dad shakes his head. 'Nothing. Ignore me.'

'I bet it was her next door!' Pa says, gesturing to

our neighbour's house. 'She's always in her garden, smoking! I bet she was having her first cigarette of the day and some ash blew over the fence. I've got half a mind to march over there and –'

'No!' I exclaim. My dads look at me. 'I mean, you *could* go next door and give her a mouthful, but you haven't got any proof. She'll just deny it.'

'Charlie's right,' says Dad, then he reaches out to pluck an unrecognizable black shred from the line. 'It could have been worse, you know. It's just a few socks and towels. Shame I can't install a Heat Hunter Three Thousand out here.'

'Forest fires start with just a few leaves!' Pa snaps, and then he stalks back into the house.

Dad looks me up and down. 'Are you hurt?'

I shake my head. 'I'm fine.'

'Are you sure? You look a bit pale.'

'Dad, I'm fine!'

'It's OK to be a bit scared, you know. That was a frightening –'

'Dad, I'm not scared!'

He sighs. 'All right, all right.' He pauses, his gaze landing on something near my feet. 'Charlie, why is there a stuffed frog out here?'

Becoming a hermit for the weekend may be the only sensible option, but it isn't as easy as I'd hoped. Pa's voice flutters up from the garden at noon, and my stomach fills with dread.

'Charlie, come on – it's time to get ready!'

Cadno, who's draped across my chest, instantly jolts into a sitting position. I can feel the beginnings of a grumble vibrating in his belly. '*Shh*,' I mouth. Then I call down, 'Uh, ready for what?'

'It's Saturday,' Pa calls back. 'It's shopping day!'

Argh. I completely forgot that Saturday is food-shopping day. Usually, I'm happy to go because Pa lets me pick some treats and desserts, but today, well . . . not so much.

I roll over to the edge of the platform. Pa is standing at the back door.

'Do I have to come?' I moan. 'I'm eleven! I'm

old enough to look after myself.'

'You said it yourself,' says Pa. 'You're eleven. Hurry, go and get ready.'

'But, Pa –'

'Listen, either you come shopping with me, or you go to visit your grandmother with Dad, but you are *not* staying at home on your own.'

I pause. Gran lives in a residential home for elderly people. Her room is small and cramped and filled with flowery furniture. There's barely enough room for a hamster, let alone a fox cub who could burst into flames at any moment.

I guess I have no choice.

Twenty minutes later, I'm sitting bolt upright in the back of the car with a demented smile on my face. My attempt at looking relaxed isn't really working.

'Do I smell or something?' asks Pa, meeting my gaze in the mirror.

'What?'

'You've decided to sit in the back, when there's room in the front. I just wondered if maybe it's because I smell. It's a joke. Charlie, are you all right? You seem a bit . . . tense.'

Well, that might be because in the backpack between my legs I've got a firefox who might erupt into terrified flames if we go over a speed bump.

'Tense? Me?' I laugh, perhaps a bit too loudly. 'I don't know what you're talking about! I'm absolutely fine. I've never been so fine!'

Pa raises an eyebrow. 'Er, OK.'

An amber eye peers at me through the gap in my backpack's zip, followed by the beginnings of a squeaky whine. My eyes widen in alarm.

'The song!' I blurt out, flapping my hand at the radio. 'I love this song! Please could you turn the volume up?'

Pa frowns. 'I didn't know you liked rap music.'

'Er, yeah, I love rap.'

'*Oooo-kay.*'

Pa turns up the volume and fills the car with beat-heavy music, drowning out Cadno's whining. I reach down and pet him through the gap in the zip. His fur is warm, as always, but there's not a flame in sight. Even so, I can't relax.

We pull into a parking space at the supermarket five minutes later. Pa gets out of the car, but I don't move.

'Charlie, are you coming?'

'Oh, I thought I might stay in the car,' I reply.

Pa scowls. 'It's, like, a million degrees. You can't stay in there.'

'I'll be fine.'

'I don't know what's got into you today, but this isn't up for debate. Shift your butt.'

I groan, scoop the bag on to my back and slip out of the car. I can feel Cadno's warmth through the fabric as Pa grabs a trolley and wheels it towards the automatic doors.

As we pass through, I glimpse a sign on the glass:

GUIDE DOGS ONLY

It doesn't say anything about firefox cubs. I keep walking, past a store assistant building a pyramid out of toilet rolls. It's already reached his shoulder.

Pa leads the way down the aisles. I trail behind at a safe distance, careful to weave round anyone and anything. Every now and then, I pause to pat Cadno in the backpack, just to keep him happy.

It's all going very smoothly. Maybe we can do the whole shop and get home without anything weird happening.

'I just remembered – we need new socks after what happened this morning,' Pa declares suddenly, wheeling the trolley round.

'I'm just gonna go for a wander,' I reply. I need to stick to the quieter aisles, where nothing can frighten Cadno and trigger his fire.

'All right, I'll text you when I'm at the till,' says Pa, and off he goes.

I heave a sigh of relief. For now, we're completely alone.

I meander round the store, passing the bakery.

'Excuse me.'

I leap with fright as I turn round – but it's only an elderly lady. She looks up at me hopefully, her eyes enlarged behind her glasses.

'Er, hello,' I say.

'I was wondering if a tall young man like yourself wouldn't mind getting a jar of gherkins for me?' she says with a kind smile. 'They put them so high up.'

I really don't want to. I want to stay away from everyone. That's the only way to be safe. But what sort of monster would I be if I denied this lady her jar of gherkins?

'Yeah, OK,' I say. She beams and leads me down the nearest aisle.

'There they are,' she says, pointing to the top shelf.

I get on to my tiptoes and reach up, keen to get the whole thing over with as quickly as possible. My fingertips graze a jar.

'Do you know that your bag is open, dear? Here, let me close it –'

My eyes widen. 'No!'

I whirl round, but it's too late. Cadno, alarmed by the appearance of a pair of gigantic bug eyes right above him, leaps through the gap. My bag is almost torn from my back with the force of him flying out and hurtling across the aisle like a comet.

The old lady cries out as Cadno whizzes by. I feel bad, but I don't have time to help her fetch her gherkins. I chase after Cadno, zooming down the aisle and skidding round the corner like something out of a racing video game. My trainers screech against the floor.

Cadno is nowhere to be seen. I stand still and wait – for the sound of screaming, or for the scratch of smoke in my throat. Something, *anything*, that will indicate where he is. How hard can it be to find a fox cub in a supermarket?

I start moving again, my mind aflame with terrifying thoughts. What if Cadno has already

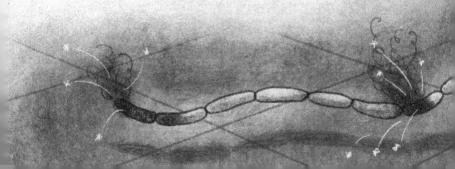

slipped through the entrance and is wandering around outside? What if he sets fire to something? What if I never see him again?

But then I turn into the topmost aisle of the shop, the one that runs along the back wall, and there's Cadno – and he's glowing.

He's prancing away from the fresh-meat counter with something clamped in his jaws. Something that trails along the ground behind him like a length of rope while his tail swishes proudly in the air. Then the smell hits me. The delicious aroma of something cooking, something that smells a bit like . . .

'*Sausages*,' I whisper, unable to believe what I'm

seeing. Cadno has pinched a string of raw sausages and now they're sizzling in his jaws as he makes his escape! The lady working behind the meat counter has her back to us, and I desperately hope she doesn't turn round and see a fiery fox cub making a getaway with her sausages.

'Cadno!' I hiss, and then he spots me. His ears droop. His tail stops swishing. Busted.

Cadno drops the sausages and bolts down the nearest aisle. I chase after him, hopping over the trail of sausages as I go. A few shoppers leap out of the way as he barges past, their faces aghast. I wonder what they must think, but I'm hoping not to be around to explain.

He keeps going, running towards the automatic doors at the entrance. I pump my legs faster. I reach out, hurl myself forward, my arms closing round him. Cadno lets out a grunt, the heat of his fur just about bearable, and we go sliding across the floor. A shadow looms over us, something tall and pyramid-shaped.

'Oi!' a voice calls, but it's too late – we crash

through the wall of toilet rolls that the shop assistant was building near the entrance. The whole thing collapses, squishy cylinders tumbling round my ears. We skid to a halt, buried underneath a mountain of loo rolls.

It's a soft landing. I want to stay under here, where it's squashy and warm, with Cadno held against my chest, and pretend none of this ever happened. I don't want to face what's coming next.

He licks my cheek, as though to say sorry. I ignore his kisses and hurriedly coax him back into my backpack before emerging from the wreckage.

There's a crowd of people gathered round the ruined toilet-roll display. The shop assistant has his head in his hands.

'That took me hours!' he groans.

'Charlie?'

I turn round and there's Pa, carrying bags of shopping. He looks confused, as though he can't quite believe what he's seeing.

'Er, I can explain,' I say, when I really can't. I

haven't the faintest clue how I'm going to get out of this one.

'Excuse me, sir,' says a man in a black blazer, stepping through the crowd. 'Is this your son?'

Oh great. Security. I hope nobody mentions that they saw a fox cub running about. Perhaps we got lucky. Apart from those shoppers in the aisle, perhaps it all happened too quickly for anybody to notice.

'Yes, he is,' says Pa through a grimace.

'I'm going to have to ask you both to leave the premises,' says the security guard, and Pa stalks forward. Despite the circumstances, I do feel a rush of relief that nobody has mentioned a stampeding fox.

'Don't worry, we're leaving,' says Pa. 'I apologize for the mess we've caused.'

We make our escape. I have never wanted to be swallowed by the ground more in my life. Cadno squirms and wriggles in the bag.

I wish it was tomorrow already, so I could have my normal life back.

Chapter 8

Twenty-one hours. That's how long is left until Teg
returns for Cadno.

We're back in the tree house. I'm lying against my
beanbag, running my hand from between his ears all
the way down to his tail. He leans into each stroke, his
eyelids drooping blissfully.

'Charlie?'

It's Dad. I army-crawl to the edge of the platform
and peer down. Dad is standing there in a T-shirt and
jogging bottoms.

'Hi,' I say gloomily.

'Pa told me about what happened in the supermarket,' he says. 'Do you want to talk about it?'

'It was an accident,' I say. 'I slipped and fell. I said sorry to Pa on the way home. For getting us into trouble.'

'I know, and Pa isn't angry with you. You didn't do anything wrong.'

When I don't reply, Dad goes on.

'I came to ask for a favour. I need you to help me fetch something from the attic.'

'Oh.'

'Your enthusiasm is overwhelming, Charlie.'

'No, no, it's fine,' I say. 'I'll be down in a sec.'

Dad goes back in the house, and I turn to find Cadno nestling into the beanbag, exhausted by his supermarket rampage. He may have an appetite for carnage, but thirty minutes of frantic playing means he then sleeps soundly for an hour. He doesn't wake even when I pick him up. He's snoring – squeaky, almost piggish little grunts. He'll be safe up here.

'I'll be right back,' I say, even though he's not listening. I just hope he doesn't sleepwalk.

'What are we fetching?'

I watch as Dad ascends the ladder into the attic.

'Your old baby stuff,' he replies. 'We're going to start making the spare room look more like a nursery.'

My stomach clenches. With everything that's been happening, I'd completely forgotten about getting a little brother or sister.

'Oh right.'

Dad's head reappears in the gap and he beckons me up.

I feel tense as I climb the ladder because I know Dad is about to try and talk to me about feelings, which I never find easy.

I heave myself into the attic. There are boxes full of Christmas decorations, old CDs, photo albums and videotapes, all coated in dust.

'I want to get your cot,' says Dad, pointing to

some slats of wood and foamy fabric in the corner. 'Gimme a hand, will you?'

I help him pull the different pieces out, waiting for the moment he's going to spring a parent-talk on me.

Once we've got all the bits piled up, it happens.

'So, what do you think about Pa and me adopting another baby?'

Silence. I know the answer he'd *like* me to give, but does that mean it's the *right* answer?

'I think it's amazing,' I say, plastering a smile on to my face. 'I've always wanted a little brother or sister.'

'You're not just saying that to keep your dads happy?' he asks. 'Because you haven't *seemed* all that pleased since we told you, you know. You've been acting differently.'

'I've just had a few things going on with school,' I reply. There's no way I can tell him that the real reason I've been acting differently is curled up in a ball in the tree house.

Dad's expression softens. 'Do you want to talk about it?'

I hesitate. 'Well . . .'

He looks at me encouragingly.

'Dad, how are you so brave?'

'What do you mean?'

'You're a firefighter. You do dangerous stuff every day. I could never be brave like you,' I mumble.

Dad smiles and puts a hand on my shoulder. 'Just because I'm a firefighter doesn't mean I don't get scared. Believe me, I get scared all the time. I just don't let it control me. I make sure I control *it*, see?'

I nod slowly.

'There's no such thing as bravery. It's all just pretending. It's being scared of something and standing up to it anyway. Where has all this come from, Charlie?'

Where do I start? I'm hiding a fugitive firefox cub in my tree house and I'm scared of the chaos he's brought with him. I'm scared of being a big brother and not being able to protect my sibling because

I can't even protect myself . . .

'Is this all because you're going up to secondary school in September?'

Oh yeah. That too.

'Yeah, a little bit,' I reply. At least that's *one* of the truths.

'Listen, your inner fire is in there,' says Dad, and he prods my chest with his finger, just over where my heart is. 'Just waiting to come out. It's the only fire I'll ever encourage you to start.'

We share a silence, in which we both stare down at our hands.

'Anyway,' Dad goes on, 'Pam is coming back on Wednesday afternoon. She might want to take a look round the house or have a talk with you. Do you think you'll be OK with that?'

I nod. Cadno will be gone by then. Normality will have returned. Dad's eyes are twinkling in that dreamy way that you sometimes see in cartoons. My dads really want this baby. I do too. I just need to figure out how to be a good brother first.

★

Later that evening, a message pings through on my phone. It's Lippy. She's sent a message to our group chat.

Lippy: *Shall we do something tomorrow?*
Roo: *Ooh yes!!!*

I chew my lower lip before typing back my response.

Sorry, guys, I can't do tomorrow!! Got a family thing going on.

I feel an immediate pang of guilt. Lippy, Roo and I very rarely go a weekend without seeing each other. And they would adore Cadno. Lippy's from an animal-loving family and Roo has always wanted a dog – which is basically what Cadno is, except a bit warmer. He is, quite literally, a hot dog.

I want nothing more than to share him with them,

but what's the point when he's going home tomorrow? They'd get so attached, only for me to take him away again. It'll be difficult enough for me to say goodbye, even with all of the stress he's caused.

Lippy: *Awhhh, you're no fun* 🙁
Roo: *You're being weird, Challinor!*
Me: *I'm not being weird. I really do have plans!*

I don't tell them that my plans involve hiking back up to the castle, meeting a boy from a distant magical realm and handing back the firefox cub I've been babysitting.

Lippy: *Hmmmmmmmmmmmmmmm.*

I puff out my cheeks, and then a thought occurs to me.

Me: *I forgot to tell you guys, I hid the next pebble.*
Lippy: *You did???*

Roo: *Great, so it goes on.*

Me: *Want the clue?*

Lippy: *Yes!!!!!*

Me: *To find the pebble, you need to head north-west.*

A pause. Lippy is the first to respond.

Lippy: *Clever, Charlie. Very clever . . .*

Roo: *Ugh. Is it too late to stop being friends with you?*

Me: *Yup! See you both on Monday.*

Our conversation ends, and I look up. Cadno is leaping round the tree house, chasing after a tennis ball. His body ripples with excitement, his goofy paws batting the ball across the floor and his fur just beginning to glow like embers.

After about ten minutes, he collapses on to my feet, panting. He feels toasty through my socks.

'Had enough, have you?'

Cadno licks my sock in acknowledgement, and then wrinkles his nose.

'Yeah, I can't imagine that tastes too good,' I laugh, and then I bend forward to stroke his head.

This time tomorrow it'll all be over. Cadno will be back in his homeland and it will be as though none of this ever happened. It's been a crazy twenty-four hours. Cadno has stampeded into my life, burning it all up and making it into something new. Something chaotic.

And, while I can't wait to get my normal life back, I still have a sinking feeling at the thought of handing him back to Teg tomorrow. He's good company – even now, as he does a poop in the middle of my tree house.

Chapter 9

By half past eleven the next morning, Cadno's melted a plastic Tarzan figure, ripped a foam dinosaur to shreds, and burned a stuffed dragon from the inside out.

Still, it's with a heavy heart that I scoop him up in my arms and tuck him into my backpack.

'Come on, then. Let's get you home.'

In the front garden, Pa is leaning over the hedge to talk to our neighbour, Jerry.

'That's what Mrs Number Thirty-Six said,' Jerry

is saying as I make my way down the garden path. 'Just roaming the streets. A huge black dog. Bigger than a wolf, she said.'

That's when I stop walking.

'Oh, Charlie,' says Pa, noticing my presence. 'Where are you off to?'

'I, er . . .'

I can't think what to say. I'm still stuck on what Jerry just said: a *dog* roaming the streets. I remember that howl I heard two nights ago, and what Teg said about the creature he was running from, the Grendilock.

It can take many forms, its favourite being the hound.

Could it be?

'Charlie?'

I shake my head. 'I'm . . . er, I'm going up to the castle with Lippy and Roo.'

Pa nods. 'OK, well . . . be careful, won't you?'

I wave goodbye and hurry down the path, my mind racing. They can't have been talking about the Grendilock. It must just be a stray dog someone's spotted. And the howl – that could have been somebody's pooch singing away in their garden. A really eerie ghost pooch. There's no way the Grendilock is prowling the streets of Bryncastell. Teg closed the gateway after him. I *saw* the wall reappear.

We arrive at the castle a few minutes before midday. There's no one about, so I fish Cadno out of the backpack and put him down. Immediately, he starts bouncing around, relishing the freedom. I laugh as he chases a butterfly.

I half expect to see Teg already waiting for us, but, when we round the curve of the north-west tower, the clearing is empty. The summer breeze brushes through the curtain of ivy, revealing glimpses of blackness behind it. The gateway is open. But Teg is nowhere to be seen.

I turn in a circle, searching for a hint of movement.

'Teg?'

The word echoes round the clearing, ricocheting off the walls, but nobody answers.

Teg isn't here. My stomach starts to squirm. Something doesn't feel right.

I glance at the time on my phone – it's a few minutes after midday. I don't think Teg's the sort of person to be late. I step towards the ivy, observing the slivers of black between the ropes of greenery. The gateway leers at me.

And that's when I see the marks in the ground. Except they're more than just marks – as I creep closer, I realize that they're more like gouges. Long, violent slashes that lead from the darkness behind the ivy. It's as if something enormous, something *dreadful*, dragged itself out of the gateway and into our world. Something with claws the size of kitchen knives.

I follow the gashes into the middle of the clearing, where they trail away, their shape changing. They

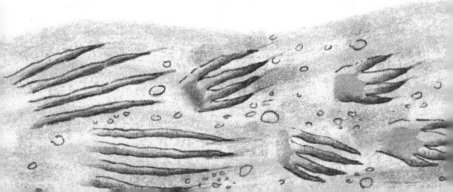

get less deep and narrow and become rounder – like footprints.

I let out a cry when I realize what I'm looking at.

They *are* footprints. But they're not human footprints. No, these are pawprints, and they look like they belong to a dog – a hound. And, judging by the size of them, this particular hound is *gigantic*.

I remember the howls that came through the gateway the night I met Teg. I think back to the conversation I just heard between my pa and Jerry about a big black dog roaming Bryncastell.

Maybe the howl I heard that first night in the tree house wasn't a dream after all. Maybe the Grendilock really is here, prowling the streets in the shape of a terrible hound. A hound . . . perfect for hunting foxes.

But how could the Grendilock be here? I saw the gateway close behind Teg.

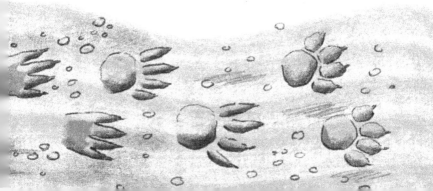

I feel a hollow sensation in the pit of my stomach as the realization creeps over me. I might have seen the gateway close, but I have no way of knowing what happened afterwards, on the other side. What if the Grendilock got hold of Teg and took the sealstone? Because, if Teg isn't coming, that means Cadno is stuck here, with me. On our own.

At my feet, Cadno growls – except this one isn't playful. I can feel his heat licking at my legs as his anxiety grows, and within seconds his flames emerge. He presses his nose to the ground and starts to sniff, his body twitching jumpily as he approaches the pawprints.

'What is it, boy?' I glance about the area, expecting to see a monstrous hound rounding the corner.

Whatever's happened here, Cadno doesn't like it – so much so that he starts barking.

'Cadno, no! *Shh!*' I hiss, rushing forward, but the heat of his flames stops me short.

His barks are basically squeaky little yaps, but it doesn't matter. If it *has* slipped through into our world, then the Grendilock could be anywhere. It could be watching us right now, waiting to pounce.

'Cadno, please be quiet,' I plead. He must sense the desperation in my voice because he quietens down, his tail drooping between his legs.

'OK, let's go,' I mutter, chills shooting up and down my spine.

I turn and run, with Cadno at my heels, leaving the gateway and those jagged slashes in the earth behind.

I don't stop running until we're at the bottom of the hill, and only then because my lungs are on fire.

'It's OK,' I tell Cadno. 'You're safe. We're safe.'

Admittedly, I don't sound too sure. Cadno sidles closer to me, his tail flicking apprehensively. Even though his flames have shrunk away, he still feels hot. Alert.

I straighten up, my mind racing. What am I going to do? Where's Teg?

Something must have delayed him. There's no way Teg wouldn't turn up to retrieve Cadno. But what if Teg comes looking for him now? How will he know where to find us? I daren't go back to the castle again, not now I suspect the Grendilock has been there.

But then I remember something. Something I've been carrying in my pocket for the last two days.

I pull out the pennycog, its toothy golden cogs gleaming. I take a deep breath, then wind them up. When I let go, the cogs unwind for what feels like an age before slowing to a standstill.

It will lead me to you, wherever you are, Teg said.

So, if it's working properly, right now, wherever he is, Teg's own pennycog should be starting to whirr, pointing in our direction like a compass.

I look back up at the castle, half hoping to see him come bounding over the drawbridge straight away.

When he doesn't, I put the pennycog away. *He'll come*, I tell myself. Right now, we just need to put a safe distance between us and the castle.

I glance down at Cadno. He's staring up at the castle, too, a whine lingering in his throat.

Suddenly I feel giddy. Until this moment, I knew he was leaving and life was going to return to normal. But now I have no idea how or when or even *if* he's going to get home, and there's no escaping it.

I've got a firefox cub in my care.

I can't keep him hidden forever. That's impossible. He's too wild a fire for me to contain on my own. If I'm going to keep him under control, I'll need help.

But there *is* somebody I could tell. Two somebodies actually. Now that Cadno and I are stuck together for the time being, I could definitely use their help in keeping him a secret. I don't have to do this alone.

I pull out my phone and type out a quick message:

Plans have changed. Meet me at my place. I've got something MAJOR to show you.

The responses are immediate.

Lippy: *So we're your backup plans??*
Roo: *Look who's come crawling back!!!*
Me: *GUYS. YOU DON'T WANT TO MISS THIS.*

The replies take longer this time, but it's Roo who responds first.

Roo: *OK, you got me with the ALL CAPS! Be there in twenty.*
Lippy: *No need to shout! But yeah, I'll also be there in twenty.*

I muster a smile. 'Come on,' I say to Cadno. 'Let's get you home. I've got two people I'd like you to meet.'

Chapter 10

I've barely collapsed on to a beanbag when a familiar bird call trills from below. Cadno snaps to attention, barking squeakily, with the front half of his body pressed against the floorboards, his paws splayed wide.

'*Nonono!*' I groan, pulling him close to me. His fur is heating up, just starting to glow, almost too hot to touch – but I manage to get him to stop barking by running my hands from his ears to the base of his tail. It seems to be his favourite.

'Come up, quick!' I urge, my heart hammering as the ladder creaks.

This is it. I'm about to share the biggest secret I've ever kept – perhaps one of the biggest secrets anybody has ever kept in the whole world – with my two best friends.

Lippy's head appears, followed by her body.

'Charlie,' she says. 'What was that noise? It sounded like a dog.'

Roo is next, his face alight with excitement. 'Did you guys get a dog?'

'Oh my gosh, you've got a puppy, haven't you?' Lippy exclaims as she helps Roo on to the platform. 'This is the best day ever!'

Lippy turns to face me, Roo looks up – and both of their gazes land on Cadno at the same time. Their mouths drop open in unison.

'A *fox* –' Lippy starts.

I bring a finger to my mouth, silencing them. Cadno tries to hide by burrowing his snout into my armpit. I get it – I'm shy around new people, too.

'Please don't freak out,' I say. 'My dads don't know about him.'

Lippy's hand flies to her mouth, like she has to stop the squeal from tumbling out.

'Is *he* . . . is he the surprise?' Roo stammers.

I snort. 'Is he not surprising enough?'

Roo quickly shakes his head. 'Oh no, he's definitely surprising.'

'Guys, meet Cadno. Cadno, meet Lippy and Roo.'

Cadno refuses to peer out from his hiding place.

'Charlie . . . have you realized that he's, er . . . *glowing*?' Lippy whispers. Her face is basking in Cadno's warm orange halo. 'Please tell me you're seeing this, Roo.'

'Oh, I'm seeing it.'

'Erm, yes,' I reply. 'That's right. You see, Cadno's not your normal fox. He's actually a firefox. The glowing is completely natural. It just means he's a bit nervous.'

Lippy takes a deep breath. 'Charlie, what the heck is going on?'

'Start from the beginning, and don't leave *any* details out,' adds Roo.

I sigh before launching into my story. I tell them first about how Teg burst through the curtain of ivy up at the castle, and how he was only supposed to leave Cadno with me for a couple of days. I tell them how Cadno's fire is governed by his emotions. I tell them about the Grendilock, and about the hound that's been seen roaming the streets. Lastly, I tell them that Teg didn't turn up to collect Cadno, so it looks like I'm stuck with him for a while.

By the time I'm done, Lippy and Roo have pulled their beanbags closer. Cadno peers nervously at them from my lap, his glow highlighting their bewitched expressions. From where I'm sitting, it looks like they've opened a chest of pirate treasure, dappled gold dancing across their features.

'So this is for real?' Lippy asks.

'I know I've got an active imagination, but I don't think even I could make all of that up.'

'He's right, mind,' says Roo. 'He's not *that* smart. No offence, Charlie.'

'None taken.'

'He's . . . he's –' Lippy searches for the right word – 'he's *adorable*, Charlie. Can I touch him?'

I feel Cadno's tail wagging against me. For the first time since Lippy and Roo arrived, he's starting to relax.

'Go ahead,' I say. 'He's a bit shy but he'll come around.'

Lippy hesitates. 'Will he burn me?'

'I don't think so,' I reply. His fur is cooler now, a pleasant warmth against my skin. 'He only burns things when he's angry, scared, hungry, or if he gets overexcited. Just be calm and slow.'

Lippy edges closer and carefully reaches out. Cadno watches her guardedly. I'm about to tell Lippy to withdraw her hand, but then he does the unthinkable – he extends his neck and licks her fingers. A few seconds later, he leans into her touch.

'He's *warm*, Charlie!' Lippy gasps in astonishment

as she ruffles him between the ears. 'It's like putting my hand into a sunbeam!'

Cadno tilts his head to the side, his pointed ears slanted floppily, and to my surprise he clambers from my lap and waddles over to Lippy. He props himself up on her knees and starts to kiss her until Lippy falls back, squealing with glee as the portly little cub climbs all over her.

'Charlie, he's amazing!' Roo smiles as he joins in. Cadno can't seem to decide how to divide his time fairly between them, so he flits from one to the other like a lovable meteorite. A kiss for Lippy, a kiss for Roo. His fur is shimmering again, but this time it's with excitement rather than anxiety.

'I'm glad you like him!' I laugh along with them. 'He definitely likes *you*!'

They carry on like this for another few minutes. Finally, Lippy and Roo crawl away, both of them panting, exhausted from all the laughter. Cadno trots over and plants a sloppy wet peck on my arm, as though to tell me that he hasn't forgotten about me.

'Charlie, he's incredible!' Lippy pants. 'You're so lucky you get to look after him!'

'Actually, that's sort of why I let you in on the secret.'

'What do you mean?' asks Lippy, and then her face lights up. 'Ooh, do you need babysitters? Because I am definitely on board for that!'

'Sort of,' I reply. 'It's just that summer's about to start, and if I didn't tell you about him I'd have to keep him a secret and probably avoid you both the whole time. Now that you know, I was hoping you could help me look after him. Especially if there might be a monster wandering around, looking for him.'

'You don't know for sure that the Grendilock thing has come after him, though, do you?' says Lippy. 'That dog people have seen could just be somebody's lost pet.'

I shuffle about uncomfortably. She's got a point – but I can't help feeling that she's wrong on this one. There was something so unnatural about the howl I heard. Something *wrong*.

'Besides, didn't you use that thingumajiggy?'

'The pennycog,' I put in. 'Yeah, I did.'

'Well then, Teg should get here soon. Until then –'
Roo grins – 'we'd *love* to help! I'm an expert
babysitter.'

'I mean, that sounds great, but there's just one
small problem.'

'What?' Lippy and Roo ask in unison.

'We still have four days before the end of term,' I
say, my breath catching in my throat. Tomorrow, I
have to go into a building full of other people and lots
of flammable stuff. Wooden tables. Paper. 'There's no
way I can leave him at home on his own. But I can't
exactly take him into school either, can I?'

My friends look down at the cub cradled in my
arms. His big, bushy tail flicks back and forth, and he
starts to paw at his own cheeks in a hamstersish sort of
way. He looks ridiculous.

Lippy chews her lip thoughtfully. 'Hmm, I
wonder . . .'

'Ooh, that's the face,' says Roo.

'What face?' I ask, but I'm pretty sure I know what he means. I can see it in the stitch of her eyebrows, the intensity of her gaze.

'Her thinking face,' Roo replies. 'She's cooking up some wild idea right now. What is it, Lippy?'

'Well, I think I have a plan.' She grins. 'And it's only *slightly* wild. What if we keep him at Pet Hospital?'

Lippy's mother's veterinary surgery sits in the middle of town, next to the farmers' market.

'We could sneak him in before school,' Lippy continues.

Cadno has climbed from my arms and is playing with Roo, who's wheeling a toy car across the floor and sending him into a frenzy.

'Mum's got these kennels outside where she keeps the more outdoorsy animals – you know, sheep or goats – and they almost never get used. Sometimes they're used as a pet hotel for when owners are away, though. We get lots of rabbits, guinea pigs, that sort of thing.'

'What if your mum or one of the other vets finds him?' I ask.

It's a good idea, but it makes me nervous. So many things could go wrong. Visions flit through my mind's eye, all of them filled with violent flames and all manner of pets fleeing into the streets.

Lippy shakes her head. 'Nah, some of the kennels haven't been used in years. We can make him a nice little bed, put some toys and food in there. He'll have a ball!'

'I have something that could help,' says Roo, pausing in his game. Cadno grunts in protest and paws at the air, urging Roo to keep playing.

'Go on,' says Lippy.

'Well, when my littlest sister was born, my mum used to use this camera thing to watch her while she slept,' Roo explains. 'You download an app on your phone, which connects to the camera, and then you can check in on your baby whenever you want without missing any of *Coronation Street*. You can even speak into the phone and your voice will come out of the camera. You could use it to keep an eye on Cadno.'

'That . . . that's genius, Roo!' I cry. 'Do you still have it?'

Roo nods. 'Yep. I can meet you guys tomorrow morning before school if you want, and bring it with me?'

'Roo, you're amazing.'

Lippy clears her throat.

'You're amazing, too, Lippy,' I say. 'In fact, you're both amazing and I'm *really* glad I introduced you to Cadno. I don't know how I'd get through the next few days without you.'

'Pfft!' Lippy scoffs. 'It looks like you were doing

a pretty good job with him on your own. You should be proud of yourself.'

I look up, my heart swelling. 'You think?'

Lippy meets my gaze. '*I know.*'

She's right. Looking after a firefox cub is no easy feat, and I've managed it single-handedly for nearly two days! Maybe my inner fire really is starting to catch.

My friends grin. Cadno has taken matters into his own paws and snatched the car from Roo. He's trotting proudly around with it clamped in his jaws. I laugh, and then we're all laughing.

Later that evening, I lie in my bed and stare up at the ceiling, Cadno propped next to me, his head resting on my chest.

'We're going to get through this,' I say. 'We've got Lippy and Roo now; they'll help us. We've got nothing to worry about.'

He doesn't answer. Of course he doesn't: he's a firefox. Maybe I'm talking to myself more than him.

Because really, even with Lippy and Roo helping, there's still *lots* to worry about, and I don't know how I'm supposed to get through it all.

Cadno clambers down to the bottom of the bed and nestles between my feet and the bedframe. Within seconds, he's snoring, the warmth of his fur giving each of my toes a tiny hug.

I pull out the pennycog and hold it in my palm. I keep on expecting to hear fingers drumming on my window, to see Teg's face peering in at me. But it doesn't happen. I turn the cogs again and let them spin until they stop, then I roll over. Wherever Teg is, whatever's happened to him, I hope he can feel his own pennycog whirring in his pocket.

Cadno grunts in his sleep. I wonder what he's dreaming about. I wonder if he misses home. But, most of all, I wonder if Teg will come back soon – or if my whole world has just caught fire.

Chapter 11

I leave for school earlier than usual – and it's nothing to do with actually wanting to get there faster. No *way*. It's all part of the plan.

'Er, Charlie, are you OK? You're very early,' frowns Pa. 'Not that I want to discourage you – on the contrary, I applaud your enthusiasm. I mean, it would have helped the rest of the school year, but it doesn't matter . . .'

He's hovering by the living-room door as I hurry

down the hallway with my bag. Cadno sits curled up at the bottom. I've given him a sock to chew on, which will hopefully keep him quiet.

'Yeah, I, er . . . it's my last week of Year Six,' I say, opening the front door. 'I want to make the most of it.'

That might be a teeny-weeny lie. To be honest, I've barely spared school a second thought over the last few days. I've been a bit busy, to say the least.

First I take Cadno to a park, where I let him run around for a while. It's early and there's nobody about. I throw a tennis ball and watch him bound after it, only to singe it in his excitement. Once he starts looking a bit tired, I head into town and find Lippy and Roo waiting for me at the agreed time, just across the street from Pet Hospital.

They both say hi briefly before cooing over Cadno, who licks them enthusiastically.

'Nice to see you guys, too,' I mutter.

Lippy looks up, her cheeks pink with delight. 'Oh, sorry, Charlie, it's just that you're nowhere near as cute as Cadno. No offence.'

'Yeah, no offence, Charlie,' Roo agrees.

Cadno is enjoying the attention and ignoring me completely. Charming.

'Are you guys ready or not?'

Lippy and Roo glance up, faces blank, as though they've forgotten why we're here.

'What? Oh yeah, that . . .' Lippy begins, and then she snaps to attention. 'Yes. We're ready.'

She gives Cadno a final tickle between the ears and then gestures for us to follow her. She leads us across the road, round the back of the building to a gate, and pulls out a key.

'Mum keeps spares in the house,' she explains. She turns the key in the lock, and the gate swings open. 'Quick, go through.'

We shuffle past her and find ourselves in a courtyard. The main building of the surgery looms over us. Lippy leads us away from it and towards some outbuildings at the other end. I put Cadno down so he can have a wee before we get him settled.

Lippy shepherds us into one of the outbuildings. Inside is a narrow corridor, with booth-like kennels on one side and stacked pens on the other for smaller animals like rabbits, guinea pigs and rats.

'Mum doesn't really get anything more exotic than a chinchilla,' says Lippy. 'This whole shed's not being used at all at the moment.'

We make our way down the corridor, passing empty kennels and pens. Lippy comes to a stop right at the end and opens one of the upper pens.

'He'll be safe in here,' she says, reaching in to scatter the toys that we've brought. I peer inside: it's box-like, but fairly big. There'll be plenty of room for Cadno to move around. *It's only for six hours or so*, I tell myself.

I put Cadno down inside. Immediately, his tail drops. His coat starts to glow.

'I don't think he likes it.'

'I know it doesn't seem nice right now, but just give him time,' says Lippy. 'As soon as we leave, he'll fall asleep and when he wakes up we'll be back.'

'Hmm,' I fret. 'Roo, did you bring the camera?'

Roo delves into his bag and produces a sleek white camera that can stand up by itself. He grins proudly.

'Awesome!' I say. 'How does it work?'

He presses a button and a green light flickers to life at the top. 'I charged it last night, so it should be good to go. Now we just need to find a flat surface . . .' He trails off as he glances around, and then spots a ledge halfway up the wall. 'Ah, perfect.'

He balances the camera on the ledge, angling it so that it's pointing towards the row of pens.

'That's the best I can do, I think. Have you downloaded the app?'

'Yep.' I pull out my phone and tap on the app. It brings up a familiar image: the three of us standing before a row of stacked pens, including Cadno's.

'It works!' I cry out in glee. 'Roo, I could kiss you!'

'I'd rather you didn't.'

'OK, well, how about a group hug? We're all in on this.'

We have a quick embrace, which I swiftly break

off to glance in at Cadno. He's lowered his head, his eyes blinking imploringly out at me. This must be the fox equivalent of puppy-dog eyes. It's working – I want to reach in and squeeze him tight.

'He won't be on his own,' says Roo, and he nods his head at my phone. 'Press that button there, speak into your phone and your voice will come out of the camera.'

'Guys, we need to get going,' Lippy says. 'School starts in ten minutes.'

We begin to walk away, but I can't fight off the pang of unease in the pit of my stomach. I glance over my shoulder, but Roo steps in front of me.

'Don't look back,' he says. 'It'll make it harder. Just leave without making a fuss.'

I start to answer, but of course he's right. I straighten up, and we slip out of the building. Lippy closes the door behind us, leaving Cadno alone.

Chapter 12

The day that follows is the slowest I've ever experienced. I spend each lesson staring down at my phone, hidden under my desk, watching Cadno's every movement. He spends a lot of his time sleeping – although he does, at one point, let out a sad little howl. I quickly hold down the microphone button on the app and speak into my phone.

'*Shh*, it's OK, boy,' I whisper soothingly. 'I'm here. Just go back to sleep.'

Miraculously, he seems to listen. I don't hear

another peep from him. Still, I'm out of the door and pulling my phone from my pocket as soon as the clock hits quarter past three.

'I tell you what I won't miss about Year Six is Mrs Parry eating leftover fries at her desk after lunch,' says Roo as he and Lippy hurry to keep up with me. 'She never shares.'

'I know, and she doesn't even have ketchup,' says Lippy. 'How's Cadno?'

It takes me a second to realize she's talking to me.

'Oh, he's fine,' I reply, not looking up from the screen. I can see Cadno's pen and, although I can't see him inside, it all looks perfectly normal. 'I think he's probably sleeping –'

I stop in my tracks. A shadow has appeared on the screen. It's moving down the corridor. At first, I think Cadno has escaped, but then I realize it's way too big to be him. Fear creeps over my skin like frost. There's something in the outbuilding with him.

'Guys,' I whisper, barely able to breathe.

It's too dark to see exactly what's casting the

shadow, but it's moving on all fours and it's *huge* – about the size of a pony. It prowls down the corridor slowly, every step taking it closer to Cadno . . .

'Is that a . . . dog?' Roo frowns over my shoulder.

I shake my head. I know exactly what it is.

'It's the Grendilock!' I exclaim. 'Quick, we have to help Cadno!'

I'm about to run, but Lippy grabs my shoulder. 'Charlie, wait. We don't know what we're going up against. That . . . that *thing* looks dangerous.'

'What, so you expect me to just leave him?' I hiss.

But Lippy doesn't have time to answer because there's a flicker of movement on the screen. I glance down, a sickening feeling rushing up from my stomach.

We're too late. I think the creature, whatever it is, has reached the pen Cadno is in. It's hard to tell from the angle of the camera. With a low growl, it leaps up on its hind legs, enormous paws against the bars. Its coat is as dark as a starless night. It peers in, and I can barely look as I wait for what happens next.

But then something unbelievable happens: the creature lets out a piercing howl and hurls itself away from the pen. It collides with the wall, and the picture judders, tilts forward and then goes black.

'What's happened?' I cry, tapping the screen furiously.

'The camera must have fallen over!' Roo exclaims.

He's right; no matter how much I tap the screen, it remains black.

'Hurry!' I shout, and then I'm running down the street, my friends chasing after me.

Minutes later, we arrive at Pet Hospital. The gate that we entered by earlier is open and, to my horror, so is the door to the outbuilding. An icy dread fills the pit of my stomach. I think I might turn and run away. I really want to. I can't bring myself to move. Fear has rooted me to the spot. I'm just Charlie Challinor, the boy who lost a fight with a goose. How am I supposed to square up against a monster? What was it Dad said about bravery?

There's no such thing . . . It's all just pretending. It's being scared of something and standing up to it anyway.

But I can't. I can't pretend I have inner fire. Except I have to. Because, if I don't, Cadno might get hurt.

I take a deep breath and step up to the doorway. The corridor is empty.

I feel a rush of relief unlike anything I've ever felt before. I didn't realize how completely petrified I was.

I feel a stinging sense of guilt as I think of Cadno, and suddenly I find myself running down the corridor.

'Cadno!' I yell.

I stop outside his pen and feel a swell of relief bigger than the first when I see him there. He's pulled a blanket over himself, as though he's hiding. He blinks out at me, his huge eyes flitting back and forth over my shoulders, a foreboding growl starting in his belly.

'Cadno,' I sigh. 'You're safe!'

I open the pen and reach inside. His fur is hot and glowing, and there are freshly singed patches on his blanket. He must have got scared and lit up when the hound appeared.

'Yay! He's safe!' Lippy smiles, but then she pulls a face. 'Wait, what's that smell?'

I press Cadno tight against my chest and sniff. Now that she mentions it, I *can* smell something. It's like rotten meat and curdled milk, like something flies and worms would feast on.

'Ugh, do you think it was that *thing*?' Roo scowls.

I don't say anything. I'm too busy holding Cadno close, feeling his heat recede to a comfortable warmth as he calms down.

'What *was* it?' asks Lippy.

'The Grendilock,' I reply. 'Teg said it can take the shape of a giant hound. *Now* do you believe that it's here?'

Lippy starts to pace back and forth.

'We don't know for sure it was the Grendilock,' she says. 'It could have just been an ordinary dog. But then how did it find Cadno? And how did it unlock the gate?'

'Dogs love hunting foxes, don't they?' said Roo. 'Maybe it smelled him?'

'A hunter,' says Lippy quietly. 'Closing in on its prey.'

'Yeah, that's really not helping,' I reply.

'But then, once it found Cadno, why did it run off like that?' Lippy continued thoughtfully.

'Maybe Cadno burned it?' suggests Roo.

'*Maybe*,' I say, although I'm not convinced. I didn't see any flames. But I missed a lot after the camera fell over. I turn, spot it on the floor, then lean down to grab it.

'Hey, what's this?'

I straighten up. Lippy is standing by the pen right next to Cadno's. There's something sitting inside. Something small and furry – and cute.

It's a gerbil. I smile when it licks its tiny paws and ruffles its ears.

'*Tinkles*,' says Lippy, reading from a label outside the pen. 'Huh. I didn't realize that there was another animal in here. Must have missed him earlier.'

'Maybe Tinkles can tell us what happened?' says Roo. 'Why that big scary thing ran off like that?'

'That *was* a bit odd,' Lippy adds.

'Wait, so Cadno could have been found if somebody had come out to check on Tinkles?' I gasp. 'It was a good idea to use this place, Lippy, but I think we're going to have to come up with something else. Come on, let's get out of here.'

I want to get as far away as possible, in case the Grendilock returns. I want to go home and hide away from the world.

'You were really brave back there, Charlie,' says Lippy as we head off down the street. 'I've never seen you like that before.'

I don't feel brave. Maybe I was at first, but the closer we got to the outbuilding, the more that bravery dissolved away until there was nothing left but fear. Lippy and Roo don't know just how close I was to turning and running.

I hold Cadno close, so that he knows I'm sorry.

'So you really think a monster from another world has slipped through into ours?'

We're sitting cross-legged on my bed, with Cadno lying on his back in the middle. He's assigned each of us a body part to tickle: I've got his head and ears, Lippy has his belly, Roo has his back legs and tail.

('Why do I get the bottom-burp end?' he mutters.)

'Yeah,' I reply. 'It's called the Grendilock, and it's a shape-shifter, but Teg said it particularly likes to appear as a hound. *Perfect* for hunting foxes.'

It all adds up: the howl that I heard in the middle of the night, followed by the sightings of an enormous dog in the neighbourhood, then the hound-like monster in the outbuilding — it's too much of a coincidence to be anything else. And, no matter how many times I use the pennycog, Teg still hasn't returned, which must mean he's in trouble. If the Grendilock really *did* catch up with him and stole his sealstone, it could have used that to reopen the gateway.

'Well, it sounds far-fetched, but seeing as we've got this spoilt little hot dog right in front of us,' says Lippy, patting Cadno's plump tummy, 'I guess it's not completely unbelievable. So, what are we gonna do?'

I shake my head. 'I don't know. We've still got the last few days of school to get through. I can't leave him on his own again.'

Roo runs Cadno's tail through his hands. 'Yeah, but you're not thinking of taking him into school . . . are you?'

I don't say anything, mainly because that's *exactly* what I'm thinking. I know carrying Cadno around school in my bag all day sounds crazy, but what other option do I have?

'There may be something else we can do,' says Lippy.

My head snaps up. 'Eh?'

'Well, you know the old caretaker's store?'

The old caretaker's store is a glorified shed in the corner of the school playground where the caretaker used to keep a lot of her equipment. It's fallen out of use now, which would make it the perfect place to hide something.

Especially a refugee firefox cub with a bounty on its head.

'I don't know,' I say. 'I don't want to leave Cadno alone again.'

'But there are always people nearby!' Lippy

protests. 'PE lessons happen all day on the playground just outside . . . In fact, we've got PE tomorrow. The Grendilock wouldn't come calling with so many people around.'

'And we can use my camera again,' Roo suggests.

I take a deep breath. 'Fine. OK. At least he'll be close, and I can check up on him at breaktimes.'

'Exactly,' Lippy smiles, but then her expression turns serious. 'Charlie, we have to be careful. It's not just Cadno who could be in danger here.'

She doesn't need to explain what she means. I know that the Grendilock might try to rip through *us* to get to him.

The idea terrifies me. Just seeing that long, dark, prowling shape through the camera was horrible enough. The thought of encountering it face-to-face makes me want to crawl under my duvet and stay there forever.

But there's also a glimmer of something else within me. A spark. Because I've realized that, although I did freeze for a minute at the outbuilding, before that, while we were running over to the surgery, my first instinct wasn't my own safety: it was Cadno's. And, when I remembered he needed me, I *was* able to go inside, even if it did feel like wandering into a bear cave with both hands tied behind my back.

I think back to what Lippy said earlier.

I've never seen you like that before.

Maybe she's right. Maybe I could be a better big brother than I think. I'm not there yet, but maybe, one day soon, I could be.

Chapter 13

We meet early the next morning outside the old caretaker's store. Lippy and Roo shower Cadno with affection again before they seem to notice that I'm there.

'Sorry, Charlie,' says Roo. 'He's just so cute.'

The lock on the door has rotted away, making it easy to shove open. I build a little nest for Cadno, hide all manner of toys in among the equipment, prop the camera on top of a dusty lawnmower, then close the door and dash off into school.

The morning passes without incident. I still spend most of my time looking down at my phone, watching Cadno, but no more hounds appear. It's not until our PE lesson just before lunchtime that things start to go wrong.

Our class's teaching assistant, Miss James, takes these lessons because she's a bit sportier than Mrs Parry – well, a lot sportier. Mrs Parry has a dodgy hip. Because it's the last session of the year, she lets us do anything we want 'as long as it's outdoors and involves running around'.

Naturally, Lippy, Roo and I play football with the rest of the class as half-heartedly as possible so that nobody passes us the ball. It works – we get to dilly-dally and talk instead. The old caretaker's store lies just a few metres behind us. I have to stop myself from going over to check on Cadno whenever Miss James isn't looking.

As our classmates zip round us with the football, Lippy starts talking business.

'Now that the fete is less than two weeks away, I'm

happy to declare that, after no less than thirty-eight experimental batches, *Philippa's Phat Hamster Salad* is now ready to go global,' she says and grins. 'We need to start getting ourselves organized.'

At that moment, the ball flies towards us and we all yelp. We dive out of the way and it lands somewhere behind us. Dylan Jones waves his arms as he gallops over.

'Oi! Kick the ball back, will you?'

We exchange glances, each one full of reluctance. I'm allergic to football. Well, that's not strictly true – what I'm actually allergic to is making a fool of myself in front of the whole class by attempting to kick one.

After a few seconds, Roo huffs and gets to his feet. 'Oh fine, I'll do it.'

He cracks his knuckles and takes a deep breath as he readies himself to kick the ball back. Lippy and I watch in amusement as he takes a run-up, kicks the ball and falls over.

The ball hurtles through the air, way off to the left,

far away from our classmates. Dylan glares at Roo before running off to reclaim it.

'Sorry!' Roo calls. He doesn't look remotely as embarrassed as I would have been. How does he just not care about things like that? *Inner fire*, that's what Dad would say. He and Lippy have got tons of the stuff.

Just then, I'm distracted by something at the edge of my vision. An orange ball shoots across the field, and instantly I feel as though my whole world is about to cave in.

Cadno is racing across the field – making right for the football as it rolls across the grass!

'Charlie, what's wrong?' asks Lippy, but then one of our classmates screams and points. My friends glance in the direction of the commotion, and their mouths drop open.

'Cadno,' I whisper, and then I'm shouting: 'Cadno! Cadno!'

Suddenly I'm running towards Cadno, while the rest of the class runs in the opposite direction.

'Everyone, step away from the fox!' I hear Miss James shouting.

But I keep running. It doesn't make a difference – Cadno gets to the ball first. He clamps it in his jaws and starts leaping around excitedly. I can see his fur beginning to shimmer. He's like a ticking time bomb. Any second, he's going to burst into an excitable ball of fire. I *have* to catch him before that happens.

'Cadno!' I shout.

Cadno casts me a quick glance before bolting off across the field with the ball in his mouth. He makes directly for the children scattered across the field. I grit my teeth as they scream and dive out of the way. Cadno tears past them like a shooting star. His fur looks like it's glistening under the summer sun – but I know better. He's seconds away from putting on a firework display.

'Charlie, stop! You don't know where it's been!' Miss James shouts.

Cadno keeps running, towards another cluster of children. I see their mouths opening in horror as they disperse. Will and Zack are among them, and I feel a quick burst of satisfaction when they dive out of Cadno's way. But he doesn't stop there. He's running faster than ever, heading directly for the . . .

'Goalposts,' I hiss. 'Cadno, get back here right now!'

He ignores me, of course. I detect a flicker of motion to my left, getting bigger and bigger – Lippy and Roo.

They're sprinting across the field, into Cadno's path, arms poised to intercept him like goalkeepers, Roo on the right, Lippy on the left.

'He's yours, Roo!' Lippy cries.

Cadno speeds up, and Roo readies himself to close his arms round the runaway firecub. But there's a big flaw in Roo's goalie efforts – his legs are wide open. Just like that, Cadno zooms through them and comes

out the other side, the goalpost only metres away.

There's nothing we can do to stop him now. Our efforts are futile. All I can do is watch as he launches himself through the air and . . .

'GOOOOOAL!' cries the crowd of classmates behind us.

Cadno tears directly through the middle of the net, leaving a singed hole in his wake. I can see the flames starting to ripple along his fur. He keeps going, bounding across the grass until he disappears into the undergrowth beyond the field.

I scramble through the bushes, nettles whipping at my legs, and find Cadno sitting in the middle of a clearing. He's panting proudly, his tongue lolling and his fire twinkling as it mingles with his fur. The ball sits at his feet, sending up tiny tendrils of smoke.

'Are you serious?' I groan. 'Don't you realize that there's a monster after you? And you almost bring out your flame-thrower attack? We might as well wander around town, shouting for the Grendilock until it finds us!'

Cadno looks away, his ears drooping, and I instantly feel guilty.

'Look,' I sigh, 'let's get you back to the shed. We'll have a proper talk later. Now give me the ball.'

I lean down and scoop up the ball in one hand and Cadno in the other. His flames have died down, so it just feels like I'm carrying a hot-water bottle. He licks my cheek in apology.

I take a short cut through the undergrowth until I can see the old caretaker's store on the edge of the football field. I crouch down and hurry over to it, just out of sight of my classmates. The door is firmly closed.

'How the heck did you get out?' I mutter as I thrust it open. I glance around inside, spotting a couple of missing panes in the window. There's a stack of mouldy crates resting against the wall beneath it.

'You're too clever for your own good,' I say, and Cadno gives a boastful yap. I pull the crates away from the wall so he can't climb up to the window again. Cadno sits down in the middle of the room and stares up at me. His tail swishes back and forth.

'I'll see you later,' I say, and then I make my exit. I pull the door shut, turn round – and find Will and Zack leaning against the wall, staring at me with narrowed eyes. Will has his arms crossed.

'Whatcha doing there, goose food?' asks Will.

'N-nothing,' I say, my cheeks flushing deeply. How long have they been standing there? Did they hear me talking to Cadno? Did they see me taking him in?

'Oh really? Because it definitely looks to me like you're up to something.'

'I was . . . er . . . um . . .' *Come on, brain. Think!* 'I was looking for the ball. I think the fox must have taken it in there, dropped it and then run off.'

Will snorts and steps forward so that he's less than half a metre away from me. I can see the calculating glint in his eyes. Zack draws up behind him, craning over us both.

'I smell fox dung,' Will snarls. 'I heard you calling that fox, almost like you *knew* it.'

My words run dry. I *was* calling Cadno's name. How could I have been so stupid?

'I know you, Challinor,' Will goes on. 'You would never go chasing off after a fox like that. You're too much of a baby. *Something* weird is going on here. I don't know what it is, but I'm going to find out.'

His eyes lock on to mine, and I'm about to admit defeat and look away when a vibrating sound fills the air. Will glances down – it's coming from his pocket. He pulls out his phone and puts it to his ear, his expression smug. *Look at me getting important phone calls during school hours.*

'Hey,' he says coolly, but then his features drop when he hears the voice on the other end. He's standing so close, and the person is talking so loudly, that I can hear the words from here.

'*Wilberforce, smoochums? Just checking to see if you're enjoying your ham-and-pickle sandwiches –*'

Instantly, Will dips his head and walks away. '*Muuum*, it's not even lunchtime yet . . .'

I'm left standing in the direct line of Zack's glare,

magnified by his glasses.

'This isn't over, goose food,' he says. 'We've got our eyes on you.' He follows his leader, leaving me alone.

I should be feeling shaken. My bullies basically just told me they know I'm up to something. But one word from the whole exchange has actually made the entire ordeal worthwhile.

Wilberforce. Well, two words actually. *Wilberforce, smoochums.*

Will has never told anybody that his first name is actually Wilberforce. I think everybody just assumed it was William. Come to think of it, Wilberforce sounds a bit like a surname. It's *definitely* not your typical first name – which is probably why he's kept it a secret for so long. I smirk as I imagine what I could do with that knowledge, the power it gives me.

I'm still smirking as I wander back over to the field with the football under my arm. When my classmates see me, much to my surprise, they start clapping.

'He's got it!' somebody shouts, and then I do

something that surprises even me: without thinking, I put the ball on the ground and I kick it. It even sort of goes in the direction I intended it to – Dylan Jones only has to veer slightly off to intercept it.

I stand there, blinking in disbelief at my newfound skills as my classmates swarm round me.

'Did you chase off the fox?' somebody asks.

'Did you see it nearly bite me? It *definitely* nearly bit me!'

'You're a hero, Charlie. You saved our football!'

Among them all, Lippy and Roo grin. I have to hide my smile because this actually feels sort of good. All my life, I've avoided situations like this, but right now I'm enjoying being at the centre of things!

Miss James drifts through the crowd. 'You got it back!' she says, looking astonished. 'That's . . . well, that's the first time you've ever actually gone after a ball, Charlie. Well done.'

My cheeks go a bit red.

'Did you, er, touch that fox?' she asks.

'Erm, no,' I say. 'It just dropped the ball and ran off.'

Miss James nods uncertainly. 'OK, well, go and wash your hands, just in case. I've never seen anything like it! Wish I'd caught it on camera.'

The match recommences, and Lippy and Roo appear at my side.

'That was amazing!' Lippy beams.

'Yeah. Before-Charlie would never have done that,' says Roo.

'Before-Charlie?' Lippy asks.

'Yeah, the Charlie from before Cadno arrived,' Roo explains. 'There's no way he would have kicked the ball back.'

'He's right,' says Lippy. 'Is Cadno OK?'

'He's fine,' I reply. 'I took him back to his hiding place.'

I decide not to tell them about my run-in with Will, and the little golden nugget of information that I found out about him. That knowledge is mine for now.

Lippy smiles. 'Come on, we'd best get back to the game. I think we're gonna have to join in now, thanks to you.'

I laugh. Suddenly football doesn't seem so scary any more. It's just a ball. Besides, I've got a firefox cub in my care, and *nothing* is scarier than that.

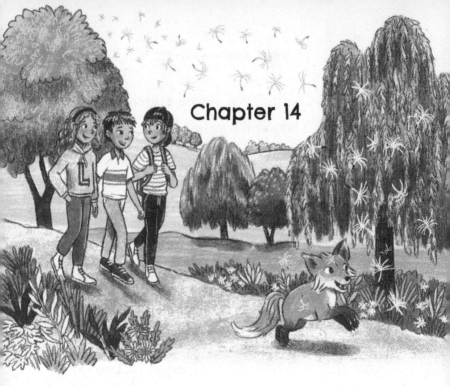

Chapter 14

I'm still in such high spirits after school that I ask Lippy and Roo if they fancy taking Cadno for a walk.

'Is that even a question?' Lippy exclaims, her eyes nearly popping out of her head with excitement.

I keep forgetting that he's still new to them. To me he's become a part of the family. A playful little fox cub who just so happens to be hiding a fiery party trick.

'So, what happens to his flames if it rains?' asks

Roo as we make our way towards the woods that border the park, after calling our parents to let them know we'll be late. Cadno is trotting happily ahead, chasing after dandelion spores as they're carried off by the breeze. We're safely away from where most of the dogwalkers go, but from a distance he'll just look like a little puppy anyway. As long as his fire stays in, that is.

'I don't know,' I admit, straightening my red-and-navy baseball cap. 'I haven't been out in the rain with him yet.'

'Ooh, what if he farts?' Roo bursts out. 'Aren't farts flammable? He could let one rip and start a bush fire!'

'I can't say I've ever heard him fart.'

'Maybe his flames are immune to his own farts,' Lippy suggests.

The rest of the afternoon passes by in a merry-go-round of exploration and laughter. Cadno chases after bugs and bounces across spongy tufts of moss. At one point, Roo throws a stick and Cadno gets so excited chasing it that it disintegrates into a heap of glowing embers as soon as he finally manages to catch it. He looks very confused and disappointed, his flames dancing about him.

'Don't worry, boy,' I assure him as his fire recedes. 'We're in a forest. It's *made* of sticks.'

We don't encounter any trouble until later on in the day. And, when we do, it comes not in the form of dogwalker or jogger but something else entirely.

We're walking round the lake when Cadno spots it. He freezes, his attention fixed firmly on something in the distance, drifting serenely across the surface of the lake. My entire body tenses.

'Oh no,' I utter. 'It's *him*.'

'Who?' asks Roo.

'The goose! The one that attacked me!'

'How do you know it's a *he*?' Lippy interjects tartly. 'Could be a *she* for all you know.'

I don't have time to answer because Cadno is already bolting to the edge of the water, a volley of yappy barks erupting from his mouth. He's glowing like a little ball of lava.

The bird — so sophisticated and peaceful when it was gliding along the water — rears up and spreads its wings, doubling in size and transforming into a feathery monster. It snaps its long neck forward, a terrifying hiss spitting from its mouth.

Cadno takes one look at it and, to my surprise, whimpers and runs in the opposite direction. The goose focuses its attention on us instead, its eyes glinting dangerously.

'Run!'

We shoot after Cadno, who's hiding just inside the safety of the woods. He's trembling like a plate of jelly. I go to pull him into a cuddle, then immediately jump back when I realize how hot he is, but there's no stifling the laughter that bubbles up from my chest.

'Defeated by a goose!' Roo roars with glee.

'Geese are, like, the great-great-great-great-grandchildren of the dinosaurs,' says Lippy. 'So he pretty much just got chased off by a modern-day T-Rex.'

'That one's got a major attitude problem,' says Roo. 'I'm not surprised you're scared of it.'

'I'm not scared of it!' I insist, but then I falter. 'OK, well, maybe a little bit.'

We laugh for what feels like an age, and walk on until the light starts to fade and the forest grows dense.

'Hey, aren't we near the old railway?' Roo says after a while.

He's right. The line is used for transporting goods – what goods, nobody knows. The track snakes through the countryside, round hills and woodlands, like a twisting silver ribbon. It's seldom used, though, which is why lots of people go for a walk along it.

'Guys, wait,' says Roo. 'Do you hear that?'

Lippy and I stop beside him. We're surrounded by trees, and all I can hear is the sound of leaves whispering, and Cadno grunting and squeaking as he plays.

'Cadno,' I hiss. 'Hush!'

Cadno falls silent, and that's when I hear it. A sound that tiptoes round the edges of things. A rasping, hungry howl that saps the warmth from the air and turns summer into winter. The noise sends a chill up my spine. The shadows that pool under the trees seem to enlarge tenfold.

'What *is* that?' asks Lippy.

It could just be somebody's dog, but I'm certain it's not. Something feels wrong. Other dogs don't sound like this. They don't sound so hollow, so soulless. There's no life behind this howl, only rage.

'I think we should go,' I say, and start stumbling backwards in the direction we came from. 'Come on, Cadno, come on, boy!'

'Wait,' says Roo, staring at something in the distance, through the trees. 'Can you see that?'

I squint and, sure enough, there's something coming towards us in the fading light. At first, I can't tell what it is, only that it's getting bigger and bigger as it stalks down the woodland path. But then it comes into focus, and my heart turns to ice.

It's a dog. A very, *very* big dog. Its fur is as black as a beetle's shell, but it's the eyes that make me realize this isn't just a normal dog: two hateful red orbs, unlike anything from this world, that pierce the growing dusk. It's advancing down the path towards us, drool dripping from its mouth. It looks hungry. No, it looks murderous.

We *have* seen this dog before.

'It's the hound,' I stutter. 'That's the Grendilock!'

'It-it's heading right for us!' Roo exclaims.

'It's come for Cadno!' I cry. 'RUN!'

We turn and bolt down the path. Cadno leads the way, yapping as he runs. His fire has emerged, his entire body enveloped in furious flames. I glance over my shoulder and, to my horror, see that the hound is running, too. Its mouth opens to reveal vicious fangs as it lets out another ravenous howl. The sound seems to drain the world of colour.

We run faster, but our efforts are fruitless. The hound draws closer with each passing second.

'Charlie!' Roo cries to my left. 'We're not going to make it!'

He's right. The hound is built for hunting: we can't outrun it. I scan the surrounding forest as we sprint on, searching for an answer –

A whistling sound shrieks in the distance, and suddenly I have an idea. It could be our only hope.

'Train!' I gasp. 'Train coming! Follow me!'

I dive to the left, off the path, my friends following me. Cadno sees that we've swerved and changes direction, too, forging a smoking path through the dense woodland.

The hound is still giving chase. Going off-road hasn't slowed it down as much as I'd hoped. The beast simply tears through the undergrowth, slipping between the trees as easily as a phantom. It won't stop . . . not until it gets us.

The train whistles again, and just up ahead I can see a clearing. We're so close.

We burst into the open, and there they are – the train tracks. Open fields stretch ahead of us on the other side of the tracks, and to our right, roaring towards us, is the train. It's enormous, a great metallic torpedo.

'Charlie, the Grendilock's coming!' Lippy cries, her voice full of desperation.

I turn to face the hound. It has slowed now, stalking us, its demonic gaze locked on Cadno. It crouches low to the ground, readying itself to attack, its fangs bared. We back slowly towards the tracks.

I glance behind me. The train is almost upon us, too, and the noise is deafening.

'Wait for it!' I scream. 'When I say go, we jump across the tracks!'

'What?' Roo shouts. 'Are you mad?'

He's right, of course. What I'm suggesting is completely foolish. Everybody knows how dangerous train tracks are. If we weren't being chased by a murderous beast, I wouldn't be suggesting it at all. 'We've got no choice!'

Cadno barks in terror. The train looms – and the hound finally launches itself at us, a hulking black

monster wreathed in the shadows of the woods.

'Go!' I yell, and Cadno vaults forward.

Together we leap across the tracks, seconds before the hound's jaws snap shut on the air where we just stood. The train thunders by, cutting us off from the beast. I look down the track, searching for the end of the train, and find none. It's a never-ending line of rattling goods trucks. We stare at it, awestruck, before I come to my senses.

'Come on, let's go!'

'Wait, Charlie!' Lippy calls, pointing at my head. 'Where's your hat?'

I frown before I realize what she's talking about. I bring my hand to my head – and, sure enough, my cap is gone.

'It must have come off when we were running,' I say. 'It doesn't matter. We need to get as far away from here as possible.'

We don't wait a second longer. We turn and flee, ducking under a wire fence and into a sloping field.

We climb up it and emerge on to a country road just as the end of the train whizzes by. The ground settles beneath our feet, but I can still feel the vibration in my bones.

I look back at the tracks and the forest beyond.

The nightmare that pursued us is gone.

'How . . . how did it find us?' Roo gasps.

We're back in town, and night is on its way. Stars glisten in the deep purple haze of the sky. Cadno is in my arms, his nose tucked into my chest. He's finally cooled down, but his fur still glimmers with trepidation.

I think back to when Teg asked for my wee-soaked jacket to lead the Grendilock away from the castle.

'Hounds have an incredible sense of smell. Cadno weed hundreds of times when we were out today. Couldn't exactly stop him, could we? I bet the Grendilock tracked us from the moment we put him on the ground.'

'What are we going to do?' asks Lippy.

I look at them hopelessly.

'I don't know. We need Teg. But, I'm telling you, something bad has happened to him. He closed the gateway after he left, but now it's open again and the Grendilock is here! It must have caught him and stolen the sealstone.'

Roo places a hand on my shoulder. 'He'll come back.'

'You don't know that. I've been using the pennycog every day and there's still no sign of him.'

To that, neither of my friends says anything. Cadno has started to chew my sleeve, oblivious to the conversation we're having about his fate.

'Come on, let's go,' I say.

Worry clouds my head as we make our way through town. What if Teg *never* comes back for Cadno?

One ray of sunshine does break through the gloom at least, and that's Lippy's words: *What are* we *going to do?* We.

It's a tiny word but an important one.

It means I'm not alone.

Chapter 15

Wednesday in school passes without incident, thankfully. I don't know how many more incidents I can take. Life with Cadno is certainly . . . exciting, to put it politely. After school, I head straight home. Lippy and Roo don't exactly grumble – they're shaken after our encounter with the Grendilock, too.

When I get there, I find a familiar car parked outside – Pam's, I realize. I'd forgotten she was visiting today. I want to sneak in and take Cadno upstairs, but Pa hears me closing the front door.

'Charlie? Is that you? Come and say hello!' he calls.

I linger in the hallway, trying to decide what to do with Cadno, then, in a moment of panic, head for the kitchen with my bag slung over my shoulder.

I open the door and pop my head in, so that it looks like it's hovering in mid-air. My dads and Pam are all sitting on stools round the table.

'Oh, Charlie!' Pam says, beaming. She's wearing a rainbow-coloured hairband that keeps her curly brown hair out of her face. 'So good to see you!'

'Er, hello,' I stammer. Cadno starts squirming in my backpack, and immediately I feel the heat rush to my cheeks.

'Aw, bless him! He looks so worried.' She laughs. 'Don't worry, love, this is only a flying visit. I was just popping by with some forms for your dads to fill in!'

She smiles at me. She's pretty much a human unicorn. I bet she even farts rainbows.

'Charlie, why don't you come in so we can talk to you properly?' asks Pa, and I can see by his eyes that it's more of a command than an invitation.

Get your behind in here, they tell me.

I smile tensely. My whole body is screaming at me to stay in the hallway and keep Cadno as far away from them as possible. But one of Pa's eyebrows quirks just the tiniest amount, and I know I've got no choice. You must never defy Pa's eyebrows.

'Oh, er, OK,' I reply, and slip through the door and into the kitchen. I just stand there awkwardly while the adults share bewildered glances.

'Anyway, where was I . . . ? Ah yes. If you could sign here, please –'

'*Meow*.'

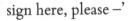

We all look up. There's a grey tabby cat sitting on the other side of the patio doors, staring in with huge green eyes.

'Aw, I love cats,' coos Pam. 'I didn't know you had pets.'

Dad sighs. 'Oh, that's Princess Cha Cha from number thirty-two. She's always sneaking into our garden. She'll go away soon.'

'Hello, sweetie!' Pam coos, hopping off her stool and going to tap the glass with her finger.

'*Meow,*' says Princess Cha Cha again. She's definitely *not* going away. In fact, she reaches up with her paw and pats the glass from the other side, so that she and Pam are doing a sort of high five.

I feel Cadno shifting against my back, his heat beginning to grow.

Oh no . . .

'I'm just going to take my bag upsta–'

'*Meow meow,*' Princess Cha Cha persists.

Cadno lets out a low growl, muffled by my bag, which begins to build until I can tell he's about to howl.

'LET'S SING A SONG!' I cry, before I even realize what I'm doing – and suddenly I'm singing 'Happy Birthday' at the top of my lungs. Anything to drown out the sound of the now-howling fox cub in my bag.

The grown-ups all turn to face me with baffled expressions. Even Princess Cha Cha stops what she's doing and quirks her head. I see her mouth open round a *meow*, but I don't hear it because I'm singing so loudly. I can still feel the rumble of Cadno's growl through my bag as he thrashes about, desperate to find out what's making that lovely meowing sound.

'*Happy birthday to yoooooouuuuuu!*'

'Whose birthday is it?' asks Pam. She's smiling in that way people do when they're a bit confused but are being polite about it.

'Lots of people's!' I shout, and then I'm *dancing*. 'Let's sing happy birthday to them all!'

My parents and Pam openly gawp at me now. They've forgotten all about Princess Cha Cha as I start stepping from side to side and clicking my fingers. I have no idea what I'm doing, but *anything* is better than them suspecting that I've got a living creature in my school bag. Even looking like an idiot.

Finally, Princess Cha Cha loses interest and slinks out of sight.

I'm singing an upbeat rendition of 'Incy Wincy Spider' now, complete with synchronized hand-clapping and foot-tapping, and I can sense that Cadno is calming down, so I gently trail off into nothingness. My heart pounds. My parents and Pam stare. My dads glance from her to me, their eyes brimming with anxiety.

She's going to think I'm bonkers. She's going to decide not to work with us any more because we're clearly a bit odd. No new baby for us. My dads are going to be *crushed* –

But then Pam gets up and starts applauding. 'Bravo, Charlie!' she cries. 'Bravo! That was just beautiful! Don't you agree?'

Pa winces when he realizes she's talking to him. He joins in with the applause, but I can tell from the way he's looking at me that he's wondering what on earth just happened.

'Oh yeah, it was, erm . . . lovely,' Pa agrees, and next to him Dad nods.

I don't know what to do, so I just sort of bow and then escape from the room with the excuse that I need a wee.

When I get to my room, I open up my bag on the bed and watch as Cadno waddles out.

'Oh, I hope you're happy with yourself!' I snap. 'You nearly blew our cover!'

Cadno grunts uninterestedly.

'You're not even sorry, are you? I don't know who you think you are. Princess Cha Cha isn't somebody you should mess with, you know? She'll have you for her supper! The Labrador at number thirty-five is *terrified* of her.'

I sigh. Now isn't the time. Pam is still downstairs.

I grab him a fistful of dog treats from my bedside

drawer. Lippy brought them into school yesterday. Cadno likes to wolf down at least four at a time. I don't blame him. I find it impossible to eat just one Jaffa Cake.

'Please be a good boy and stay quiet,' I plead with him as I head for the bedroom door. Cadno ignores me and licks the crumbs off the duvet. 'I won't be long, promise.'

I leave him and go downstairs, but, when I get there, Pam is emerging from the kitchen, her handbag swinging from her shoulder.

'Right, well, we're all done,' she's saying. 'I'll be out next week for another visit if that's OK? And I'll have a proper chat with Charlie then, too. Maybe he can give me another sing-song!'

She winks at me, and my cheeks flush deeply.

'No problem,' Dad says, grinning. 'See you next time.'

Pam gives me a wave as she opens the front door and heads down the garden path. We stand in the doorway to see her off. She gets into her car – the

one that Cadno peed on last time she visited — and drives off.

I leap back from the door with a start, a strangled cry tearing from my lips.

'Charlie?' Pa exclaims. 'What's wrong?'

For a moment, I'm unable to speak because there, glaring at me from the bushes on the other side of the road, is a pair of seething red eyes. They burn into me, filling me with their hatred. With their hunger.

And then they're gone, so suddenly that it's almost like they weren't there at all.

'Charlie,' Dad urges, 'are you OK? You've been

acting very strangely since you got home.'

'Oh yeah, I . . .' I stammer. 'I just had, er, cramp . . . in my foot, that's all.'

'Foot cramps?' Pa frowns. 'Must be from all that dancing round the kitchen. What was all that about, eh? Is it really bad?'

I shake my head. 'Nope. Actually, it's gone now. Weird, eh? Anyway, I'm gonna go back to my room for a bit.'

I can feel my parents staring after me as I go up the stairs. But I can't bring myself to worry over the feebleness of my lie because Lippy's words from the vet outbuilding are blazing in my head.

A hunter. Closing in on its prey.

The eyes are still there.

I don't mean literally – they were there for a second, and then they were gone. I'm not even sure I saw them at all, or if my imagination was playing tricks on me. But late that night, as I lie in bed with Cadno snuggled against me, I can still see them. Piercing through me like a pair of red-hot knives.

It's found me. The Grendilock knows I have Cadno because it *saw* me with him, and somehow it's managed to find where I live. Maybe it followed my scent.

The 'how' doesn't matter anyway. What matters is that the hunter has found its prey, and it's only a matter of time before it closes in. It will take Cadno, and then . . . well, I shudder at the thought of what it might do to me. Whatever inner fire I might have been kindling seems to flicker out on the spot.

So I lie there, with one hand resting on the belly of a little fox cub and the other gripping the pennycog. I wind the cogs and let them unfurl, before winding them back up again.

'Come on, Teg,' I mutter. But it's pointless. If Teg was able to come, he'd be here by now.

It looks like we're going to have to figure this out on our own.

Chapter 16

The next day is Thursday. The last day of primary school *ever*. I've been so consumed by everything that's happened with Cadno that I've not really stopped to think about that. Which is wild because a week ago it was one of the biggest worries in my life. Now it barely registers. I don't think it's anything to do with me being braver either. It's just that now I've got bigger fears to tackle. Extra pretending to do, as Dad would say.

And, while I'm on the subject of pretending, I

haven't mentioned the red eyes to Lippy and Roo because I'm trying to tell myself I imagined them. Still, as the final bell rings and I head towards the caretaker's store, I find myself glancing into the furthest corners of the school playground, searching for a pair of glowing scarlet orbs.

I let myself into the shed, where I find Cadno skittishly bouncing round a manky old mop. He looks up as I enter and barks delightedly.

He bombards me with slobbery kisses as I lean down to greet him.

'Whoa!' I exclaim. 'Yes, yes, I'm very happy to see you, too.'

He blinks at me, then starts to gnaw at my collar.

'Come on, let's get you home.'

I tuck him into my bag and make my exit. I'm almost at the gates when two arms lace round my shoulders. Lippy and Roo have caught up with me.

'I can't believe we've finished primary school,' Roo cheers. 'Secondary school, here we come!'

'Yep,' says Lippy. 'Now we're on to the next big adventure.'

I nod my head at the bag on my back, where a little firecub lies curled up at the bottom. 'We need to get through the summer first.'

'That's what I was talking about,' Lippy grins. 'I think we're in for a *very* interesting holiday.'

I try to let myself in quietly through the front door. The hallway is empty, but the door to the living room is open. I'm at the foot of the stairs when Dad pokes his head out.

'Charlie, you're home!' he says, a little more brightly than normal.

'Um, yes,' I say, coming to a stop. I desperately hope that Cadno stays quiet in my bag. 'What's up?'

'Oh, it's just that Tanya is here, so we were hoping you'd be home soon.'

'Tanya?'

'Our new social worker.'

I frown. *Where's Pam?*

Dad must be able to sense the cogs spinning in my brain because he widens his eyes at me, urging me not to question anything.

'Oh yeah – sorry, I'll just take my stuff upstairs.'

Dad smiles and ducks back into the living room. I take Cadno up to our bedroom. I dig him out of my backpack, perch him on the bed and cup his head in my hands.

'Stay up here,' I say, 'and stay quiet. I won't be too long.'

I leave the door slightly ajar and go back down the stairs, pausing to take a deep breath before entering the living room. When I do, Dad and Pa leap to their feet, both of them grinning tensely. On the sofa sits a strange-looking woman.

She's very long and narrow, a bit like a praying mantis. A praying mantis with an enormous blonde beehive hairdo. Her lips are painted the pink of cough medicine, her eyelids the blue of a peacock's feather. She's wearing a bright pink cardigan and smells extremely sweet – like strawberries, vanilla and cinnamon buns, all rolled into one overwhelming sickly scent.

'Charlie!' Pa exclaims. 'How was school?'

'Um, good,' I say, and the woman on the sofa clears her throat.

Pa's cheeks redden. 'Good, that's good. Well, we have somebody we'd like you to meet. Unfortunately, Pam has been taken ill, but we're very lucky to have already been assigned a wonderful new social worker . . . Charlie, this is Tanya Cleck. Tanya, this is our son, Charlie.'

Tanya Cleck nods, her towering beehive hair bobbing. 'A pleasure to make your acquaintance, Charlie. I came here today to introduce myself to your guardians.'

'Nice to meet you, too,' I smile as I shake her hand. Her grip is surprisingly firm.

I glance at my dads, and I can tell they're thinking the same thing. *Guardian? They're not my guardians – they're my parents.* Pa must be able to sense the unease coming from me because he gives his head an almost undetectable shake.

'So, er . . . what's wrong with Pam?'

Tanya brushes the question away with a wave of her hand. 'A truly terrible malady. She may never recover. Now let us all be seated.'

She picks up a tiny china teacup and saucer from the coffee table and takes a delicate sip. I glance at my dads. Why is she talking so funny? I don't even know what 'malady' means. They give me shrug-eyes.

'As I was saying to your guardians,' Tanya continues, setting the cup back down, 'I have come to see if this abode is a suitable place for a young child.'

I study her as she speaks. There's something odd about her. Her make-up doesn't look normal. It's more like face paint, all dried and cracked round her lips and eyes.

I smile and pretend not to notice. 'Sounds good.'

Tanya looks pleased. 'Excellent! Well, let us get started, then, shall we?'

She launches into a discussion with my dads, asking them all sorts of questions about their jobs and stuff.

It's a bit boring, but I do my best to smile and nod in all the right places. My mind wanders, and I take to gazing round the room.

Eventually, my attention lands on Tanya's feet. Her pink slip-on shoes are on wrong. I stare at them. Maybe they just look funny from where I'm sitting. I tilt my head. No – they're definitely on the wrong feet. I want to point it out to her, but I don't wish to seem rude.

And then I look at Tanya herself. She doesn't seem to be paying much attention to what my dads are saying. She keeps glancing round the room, like she's not quite sure what to make of it. In particular, she keeps shooting suspicious glares at the TV, as if she's afraid it might explode at any moment. It's like she's never seen one before.

But, after a while, Tanya smiles toothily.

'Well, that all seems in order. Now I would like a tour of the dwelling,' she says. 'Charlie, perhaps you could show me your bedchamber?'

I barely notice her weird use of words because a

roiling dread fills my stomach. There's no missing the secret that's sitting on my bed right now. How on earth am I going to explain a chubby little fox cub in my bedroom?

But I don't have time to think about it because, at that very second, a piercing scream jolts through the air. We all leap with fright.

'What on *earth* is that?' Tanya cries, clapping her hands over her ears.

'That's our new, very sophisticated, very *safe* fire-alarm system!' Dad shouts over the din. He actually looks sort of excited.

'Make it cease!' Tanya shrieks.

'We're going to have to evacuate,' says Dad, gesturing to us to get to our feet. 'I need you all to make for the nearest fire exit in a calm and orderly fashion.'

'The nearest fire exit?' Tanya stammers as Dad herds her towards the door. 'What is a fire exit?'

'The front door,' Pa explains, but his frown doesn't escape me. Who hasn't heard of a fire exit?

'Come on, everyone, stop wasting time,' says Dad. 'Just like we rehearsed!'

I wish he was joking, but Dad actually does make us do a fire drill twice a year. Last time, we achieved our personal best and evacuated in twenty-two seconds.

The noise intensifies in the hallway. The Heat Hunter 3000 screams down from the ceiling as we pass underneath, shuffle out of the front door and gather on the front lawn, or our 'assembly point' as Dad calls it.

'This is preposterous,' Tanya growls, shying away from the noise. 'Can't we just silence the wretched thing?'

'I need to establish the location of the fire,' Dad says, marshalling us into a line on the grass. He pulls out a stopwatch and then makes a face. 'Hmm. Thirty-six seconds. We're gonna have to work on that. Now, if you would all excuse me, I'm going to inspect the premises.'

And, with that, he disappears back inside. His words replay in my head, and I start to feel sweaty with panic. There's only one fire hazard in our house, and it's got four legs, a swishy tail, and it's in my bedroom *right now*. What is Dad going to do when he finds him? And what did Cadno do to set off the alarm? I can't smell any smoke.

A moment later, the alarm stops shrieking and Dad reappears. My whole body tenses up as I study his expression. But he's . . . grinning? He doesn't look like he just found a fugitive firefox cub in my bedroom.

'False alarm,' he says, waving us back inside. 'No fire. Come back inside, everyone.'

I try to maintain my composure as we head back into the house. Did he not find Cadno? But if he didn't . . . well, where is he?

'So, if there was no fire, why did that peculiar bell begin to toll?' asks Tanya suspiciously.

'The Heat Hunter Three Thousand can detect unexpected increases in temperature as well as smoke,' Dad replies, seeming not to notice her baffling choice of words. 'So it can even let you know there's a fire *before* the fire has actually started. Clever, eh?'

'Then there is something of great heat within these walls?' Tanya's eyes narrow.

'Erm, well, no, actually. But the system is still quite new,' says Dad. 'It's probably just a glitch.'

'Hmm.' Tanya marches ahead, but not before glaring over her shoulder – seemingly directly at me. I freeze on the spot.

'What was that all about?' I hear Pa whisper to Dad.

Dad shrugs. 'I'm not sure. I checked the interface, and it showed that there was a burst of heat upstairs. Only for a few seconds, and then it was gone. You haven't left your phone charger plugged in, have you?'

'Of course I haven't,' Pa mutters. Dad has strict rules about leaving things plugged in.

A burst of heat upstairs. It could only have been Cadno. Maybe something freaked him out and he let his fire erupt for a second, not long enough for anything to catch. There shouldn't be anything in my room to freak him out, but he *has* been quite twitchy since we got chased by the Grendilock . . . I'd better check it out.

I excuse myself for a toilet break and take the stairs two at a time, then freeze at the sight before me.

My bedroom door is wide open.

Chapter 17

I stop in the doorway. Cadno is nowhere to be seen. He isn't on the bed, under my desk or nosing round the side of the wardrobe.

He's not here.

This is bad. This is *really* bad. He could be anywhere upstairs, getting up to *anything*.

I go from room to room, my nerves ramping up as I push open each door. But Cadno isn't in the spare room, nor is he in Dad and Pa's bedroom or the bathroom. Nothing is sizzling; the air doesn't smell smoky. I start to worry – what if Cadno has escaped and I never see him again? But then something catches my eye.

The clean laundry basket. It sits in the corner of the landing, fresh towels piled up inside. Except the top towel has a bulge in the middle, like there's something nestled underneath.

'Why, you little . . .'

I peel back the top towel, and there's Cadno, curled up neatly among the folded towels, staring up at me with those big amber eyes. He gives me an anxious glance before trying to tunnel deeper into the towels – almost like he's trying to hide. Something has spooked him. Whatever it was, it made him explode with heat before he hid. I'm just glad he managed to reel it back in before ruining Pa's towels.

'Oi, come here,' I whisper, burrowing after him. When I manage to pull him out, the smell of Pa's sugarplum fabric conditioner clings to his fur. 'You've been very naughty. Do you realize how worried I was about you?'

I quickly carry him into the bedroom and, when I get back downstairs, Tanya is gathering up her things.

'Are you sure you've got all the information you need?' asks Pa. 'You didn't make any notes –'

'I do not need to scribe my meetings,' says Tanya through a blisteringly sweet smile. 'I have seen everything I need to see.'

She pauses and sniffs at the air. She wrinkles her nostrils.

'Er, is everything OK?' asks Pa.

Tanya flaps her hand. 'Of course. It smells terribly . . . pleasant.'

She reaches into her handbag and pulls out a bottle of pink perfume, which she spritzes herself with. It smells of vanilla, strawberries and sugar, and makes me feel a bit sick.

'An honour to make your acquaintance, Charlie,' says Tanya, her gaze landing on me.

'Erm, yeah. Nice to meet you, too.'

'And tell me, what are you going to be doing over the next few days?'

Something about her question feels sharp, like a knife edge pressed against my heart.

'Nothing really. Just helping my friends prepare for the summer fete.'

'Fete?'

'Yeah. It's next weekend.'

Tanya seems to consider this. 'So this . . . fete, it is a celebration of the season of light, yes?'

I glance at my dads, who give me urgent looks. 'I guess, yeah.'

'And you will be in attendance?'

'Erm, yep.'

'Perfect!' Tanya laughs shrilly. She breezes across the room to the front door. 'Farewell. I shall see you all *very* soon, I am sure.'

And, just like that, she's gone.

Lippy, Roo and I barely stray from the house over the next couple of days, which suits Lippy just fine because production of *Philippa's Phat Hamster Salad* is ramping up.

'We've got five days to bag up as many pouches as we can, do all the branding and put prices on everything,' Lippy declares on Monday morning as she heaves herself over the tree-house platform, lugging a hefty bag behind her. 'The fete is on Saturday, and we've got a lot of work to do.'

She opens up the bag and pulls out tray after tray of what I can only describe as green mush. Then she produces an abundance of little clear bags, decorative ribbons and reams of stickers, complete with a custom design.

'Mum and Dad got me a sticker-maker for Christmas,' she says, grinning. 'I'm so glad I've finally had the chance to use it!'

Roo mutters something about useless Christmas presents while I study the design more closely. It shows a hamster's face, its cheeks bulging with food, encircled by the words *Philippa's Phat Hamster Salad* in loopy writing.

'Aren't they beautiful?' Lippy sings.

'They're something,' says Roo.

Cadno wobbles over and sniffs at the stacks of neon-green pulp.

'Somebody thinks it smells good,' I say.

'That's because it *is* good. Now less yapping, more bagging.'

We do as we're told. Roo and I scoop handfuls of *Phat Hamster Salad* into bags before passing them to Lippy, who puts a sticker on them, decorates them with a pretty green ribbon and sets them back on the tray. Cadno bounces round us, demanding that we feed him, but Lippy refuses.

'Are you going to tell your dads about him?' asks Roo eventually.

I bite the inside of my cheek. I've been so caught up with looking after Cadno that I haven't stopped to think about it. Life with him is a daily experiment. I haven't looked past the next few days, let alone the rest of the summer and beyond.

'Um, I don't think so,' I admit.

'Don't you reckon you should?' asks Lippy. 'You

can't hide him from them forever. Especially not when he gets bigger.'

She's right. He's only been with me for a week and a half, but he's really grown. His paws are chunkier, his belly rounder, his already-perky ears even perkier. How big will he be in another week? A month? How will I keep him a secret when he's only going to get more difficult to hide?

'I know, I know. I need to tell them . . .'

'But?' says Roo. 'I can sense that there's a but.'

I hesitate. 'Well, there are two buts. The first being that I don't know how they'll react to finding out that there's a living, breathing fire hazard under their roof. My dad's a *firefighter*.'

Lippy nods. 'That is a big but.'

'Yup. Which brings me on to the second but. My dads are adopting again.'

Lippy and Roo's faces light up.

'You're going to have a little sister or brother?' asks Lippy.

I nod. 'Yeah, if all goes well. The problem is, I'm

pretty sure having a pet firefox is a big no-no when you're adopting. What if he starts a fire when the social worker comes over? What if I don't get to have a new sister or brother because of something Cadno does? My dads will be crushed. They'll never forgive me.'

Roo and Lippy's eyes fill with sympathy.

Lippy touches my arm. 'I know your dads. They're both really cool. I'm sure they would love Cadno, just like we do. Isn't that right, little firefluff?'

She leans across and runs her hands through Cadno's fur. He places his head on her palm, encouraging her to dive into a head massage.

She's got a point. Cadno is easy to love – once you get over the initial shock of his fire and all that. At some point over the last eleven days, I've come to realize that I can't really imagine life without him, even with all of the baggage he brings.

Maybe they're right. Maybe introducing him to Dad and Pa will help to ease the weight of it all.

Or maybe it won't. Maybe it will push them over the edge.

Roo nods in agreement. 'I think it's a good idea to tell them about him. That way they can help you look after him and you won't have to worry about keeping him secret.'

'Hmm,' I say. 'You're probably right. I don't know. I need to think about it.'

We return to our respective tasks. I stare into Cadno's eyes as I scoop up more *Phat Hamster Salad*. We're a unit now, but it feels like I'm living two separate lives: the normal life I have with my dads, and the life I have with Cadno – fantastical and unexpected.

Is it possible to bring the two together?

Chapter 18

The day of the fete arrives, and with it comes a heat unlike anything I've ever known. The air is soupy and still, and, though the skies are an endless blue, I sense that a storm is brewing.

Lippy arrives at my house early, with all the energy of a small hurricane. Her hair is wild and huge, her arms laden with tablecloths, wicker baskets and polka-dot bunting. Roo follows, a sheen of sweat already glistening on his forehead.

'She woke me up at half past seven,' he grumbles.

I offer him a sympathetic smile as we follow Lippy up to the tree house. She's busy assembling the pouches by size, all filled to the brim with the sticky green substance.

'Come on, we haven't got long!' she snaps. 'We need to get down there, grab our stall and start setting up. It has to look perfect by the time people start arriving. Move it, move it, move it!'

'It's just for one day,' I say to Roo as we start bunching the pouches on trays. Cadno stares at Lippy like she's lost the plot. Well, he's not far wrong.

The fete is taking place at Sunken Gardens, a public park on the edge of town. Lippy's mum, Stella, has managed to get us a stall right in the thick of it, between the baking tent and the helter-skelter.

Stella is a jovial, stocky woman with dreadlocks that go all the way down her back. She's got a nose piercing and a voice that could carry across several football pitches. Frankly, she's one of the coolest people ever.

'I've put you lot here,' she booms, pointing with a clipboard that looks tiny in her colossal hands. 'You should get a good amount of footfall all day.'

Lippy squeals with glee. 'Mum, you're the best!'

'I know, poppet,' Stella chortles. 'Listen, I'd best be off – I need to go and help set up for the Cutest Pet Competition.'

I watch as she marches off through the crowd, then feel something like a wet sponge against my elbow. Cadno is peering out at me from a canvas bag that I've got slung over my shoulder. He's been nervy all morning. He keeps jumping whenever Lippy raises her voice. He's definitely still shaken up after our run-in with the Grendilock.

'Sorry, Cadno,' I say to him. 'I think the Cutest Pet Competition is restricted to ordinary household pets, not magical creatures from a far-off land.'

Cadno growls dejectedly, his ears drooping.

'Although you would *definitely* win if you did enter,' says Roo, reaching over to stroke Cadno's ears.

We go about setting up the stall, with Lippy dishing

out instructions left, right and centre. By eleven o'clock, it seems as though the whole of Bryncastell has turned up in their shorts and sun hats. People fan themselves as they peruse the stalls. Toddlers cry out for ice cream. Children squeal with delight as they ride the bumper cars.

And business at the stall picks up. Lippy pastes on her most charming grin, and pretty soon we're selling *Philippa's Phat Hamster Salad* by the trayload. At one point, Will walks by with his mum, a glamorous-looking brunette woman in fancy sunglasses. He makes eye contact, then looks away. I feel a bubble of amusement rising up inside as I remember what she called him on the phone the other day: *Wilberforce, smoochums!*

'Oh my gosh,' Lippy murmurs, nudging me in the ribs. 'Check out that woman. She looks like a giant flamingo!'

I look up and spot who she's talking about. There's a woman wandering towards our stall who looks as though she's been wrapped in candyfloss. She's

wearing pink from head to toe, including a fluffy pink jacket that makes me sweat just looking at it, and a pair of love-heart sunglasses. She's got a stack of blonde hair that adds an extra thirty centimetres to her height.

It's Tanya Cleck.

I try to hide by dipping my head and rummaging

through the stock, but it's too late.

'Master Challinor, is that you?'

My heart sinks. I suppose it's my own fault – I did *tell* her we'd be here. I didn't expect her to turn up, though.

I emerge and smile meekly at Tanya as she comes to a stop. I can see my bewildered face reflected in her heart-shaped shades. Her face looks a lot smoother than before, like she's used proper make-up this time. Her shoes are on the right feet, too.

'Oh, Miss Cleck,' I say. 'How nice to see you!'

She flaps a hand at me. 'Pray, call me Tanya. And what produce are you selling today?'

Her eyes flit over the bags of green gunk on our table. Lippy clears her throat and leaps to her feet.

'Home-made rodent food,' she declares.

Tanya wrinkles her nose. 'Ah . . . and who are you?'

Lippy's grin fades. 'Philippa Tarquin, one of Charlie's best friends.'

Roo pops up beside her. 'And I'm Rupert Baltazar, Charlie's other best friend.'

Tanya smiles, but she looks uncomfortable. 'How . . . delightful. What did you say you are selling here?'

'Hamster food,' I reply.

'It's actually suitable for any small rodent,' Lippy interjects. 'Mice, chinchillas, guinea pigs, rats –'

'Rats?' Tanya's face twists with horror. 'You have rats here?'

'Well, not *right* here,' explains Lippy, shooting Roo and me a confused look. 'But some people in Bryncastell keep them, yeah.'

Tanya snaps her head from side to side as if she's expecting a horde of rodents to come sweeping over the field.

'Do you have any pets, then, Tanya?' I ask.

'Pets? Oh no. *Pests*, more like it,' she replies, and then her eyes narrow. 'Why, do you, Charlie?'

She's been to my house. She's spoken to my parents. She knows we don't have any pets. But there's something about the way she looks at me that pins me to the spot.

'Er, no. My dads thought it would be unfair because they both work full-time. I've always wanted a dog, though.'

Score. I deflected the question *and* made my dads sound good.

Tanya's nostrils flare. 'Hmm. So the three of you are here today *alone*?'

Lippy, Roo and I glance at each other.

'Yep, all day,' I reply.

Tanya narrows her eyes again, like she doesn't quite believe me. I pray that Cadno doesn't move underneath the table – or worse, *bark*. How would I explain that?

'Right, I shall bid you farewell.'

She reaches into her denim handbag, pulls out her bottle of perfume and spritzes herself. The air fills with that sickeningly sweet smell I remember from last time. As she puts the spray away, something slips out of her bag and falls to the ground.

'You dropped this,' I say. I lean over to pick it up and find the faded cover of an old fashion magazine staring up at me. The model on the front is wearing a pink fluffy jacket, just like the one Tanya has on. Big, bold lettering along the bottom reads *Why you should wear pink this spring*, and then I see the date in the lower corner: 1997. That was ages ago. Before I was even born.

Tanya's hand darts out and snatches the magazine from my grasp.

'Why, thank you,' she says. 'I do not wish to lose that – I do enjoy having something to peruse. Anyway, fare thee well!'

I frown after her as she spins round and vanishes into the crowd, leaving a trail of sugary fumes in her wake.

'I'm guessing that was your social worker?' Lippy says after a short while.

'Yup.'

'She seems . . . er . . .'

'Friendly?' Roo puts in.

'She's odd,' I say.

Lippy grimaces. 'Well, I didn't want to say anything, but . . .'

'Yep,' Roo agrees. 'Nobody says *fare thee well* any more.'

Chapter 19

At around midday, we have yet more unwanted guests at our stall.

'Well, well, if it isn't the weirdo brigade,' comes a drawling voice from round the corner of the food tent. Will and Zack appear, both carrying lollipops the size of dinner plates. They sneer as they take in our display.

'Oh, not you two,' Lippy groans. 'Haven't you heard? They're looking for you over in the livestock show. A pair of pigs have gone missing, apparently.'

Their smirks vanish, and I snort out loud. Will shoots me a nasty glare.

'What are you laughing at, goose food?' he snaps. 'Do you like having a girl stick up for you?'

I feel my cheeks burn, and I murmur something under my breath.

'What did you just say?' Will demands.

'Nice of you to pop over now that you've got rid of your mum,' I say, looking up. 'Why didn't you come sooner? Did you have to wait for Zack to come and keep you company?'

Will's face contorts with fury. Zack looks completely gobsmacked. Even Lippy and Roo seem a bit shocked by my retort. To be honest, I've surprised myself – but it's like I've got this newly blazing fire inside me.

'You'll regret that,' says Will. 'I haven't forgotten about the other day, you know, with that ratty little fox. I'm on to you, Challinor.'

He bangs his fist down on to the table, and a tiny bark sounds from underneath. The five of us freeze –

us in terror, and Will and Zack in realization.

'Was that what I think it was –' Will starts, but that's all he manages because a second later the table explodes away from us in a searing billow of fire. Lippy, Roo and I are sent sprawling across the ground.

I scramble to my feet. People are screaming. The fete has turned to chaos. A path has opened through the crowd, and stalls and tents have been upended, some of them smoking, as a little ball of fire shoots through the gardens.

'Cadno!' I cry.

He's been nervy for days, and Will banging on the table must have pushed him over the edge.

'I have to go after him!' I shout to my friends. 'Stay here; it's too dangerous!'

I leap over the remains of our stall and follow the trail of destruction that Cadno has left in his wake. Nothing has quite gone up in flames yet, but the grass is curling where his paws have landed. People are running around, confused, trying to salvage their stalls.

I follow his tracks to the other end of the fete, where a throng of people are fleeing out of a maze constructed entirely from bales of straw. A finger of smoke curls into the air from somewhere inside.

It looks like I've found him. I let out a groan before slipping through the entrance.

The passages are narrow. I follow the smoke, winding round and round until it seems that I'm going in circles. I hear a yap somewhere to my right.

'Cadno!' I shout. 'Stay where you are; I'm coming for you!'

But then I hear something else. A guttural, thundering bark that echoes through the maze towards me.

My heart stops. The Grendilock is here! It's in the maze somewhere, too – it's a race, and I need to get to Cadno first.

I pick up my pace. Every time I turn a corner, I expect to bump into the hound, its fangs snapping at my face. But then I take a left turn, and directly ahead of me is the middle of the maze. And, sitting at its

centre, hackles raised, is Cadno.

'Cadno!'

His head snaps round at the sound of my voice, and he zooms over to me. His flames are still bunched round him in defence, so he doesn't come too close.

'It's OK,' I whisper. 'It's OK. I'm here now.'

I start to turn, ready to find our way out before the Grendilock gets to us, when something bursts into the passageway behind us in a cloud of straw, blocking

our exit. The detritus settles, and there it stands: the hound.

It's bigger than I remember, its coat darker. It's as though it's absorbed all the shadows from the world and wrapped them round itself. It fixes me with its terrifying gaze, its eyes glowing like hot coals. I can see thick strings of drool dripping from its jaws.

I stumble backwards. There's nowhere we can go. There's only one way in and out of the middle of the maze, and the Grendilock is blocking it. Before I can stop him, Cadno bounds forward, barking, his voice tiny yet ferocious.

The hound reacts like lightning, sinking its fangs into one of Cadno's front legs and throwing him aside like a toy. Cadno hits one of the straw walls with a yelp and falls to the ground.

'Cadno!' I gasp. The little cub struggles to his feet again.

The Grendilock slinks forward, and I close my eyes, readying myself for the attack. But, before it can spring, the wall of straw to its left begins to sway. The beast turns its head, but it's too late – the bales collapse on top of it, burying the monster underneath their immense weight. I can hear its furious growling as it thrashes underneath. It won't stay pinned down for long.

'Charlie!' a voice hisses to my left, in the gap where the straw wall had been. Lippy and Roo are standing there, their faces glistening with sweat. They must have pushed the wall over, I realize. I feel a flutter of relief in my chest.

'Quick!' Lippy pants, pointing at the heaving mound of straw. 'Get Cadno to destroy it!'

'Huh?' I frown. And then I realize what she means. 'Cadno, you know what to do!'

I gesture towards the pile of straw, the hound writhing underneath. Cadno shoots me a determined glance before bounding over to the straw and whipping his flaming tail across it.

Fire spreads quickly, crackling and snapping, until the whole thing looks like a towering bonfire. The hound lets out a pained howl.

'Charlie!' Roo snaps. 'Quick, we've got to get out of here!'

He's right. The fire is spreading quickly – it's starting to crawl along the walls, the passages choked with smoke. The whole maze is going to burn from the inside out!

I whistle for Cadno. He leaps away from the burning straw and comes over to me – except there's an awkward hobble to his walk.

My stomach churns. He's hurt.

'Charlie, hurry!' Lippy calls over her shoulder. A bale of straw falls to the ground behind us, fire flickering from its underbelly. We really need to run now.

I bite my lip and pick Cadno up. His fire sears my skin, sending jolts of pain up my arms, but within seconds he cools, my touch calming him down.

We start to run, bolting down the passages as the maze crumbles behind us.

'I told you guys to stay put!' I exclaim.

'Yeah. You're welcome,' Lippy growls. 'Now come on!'

We emerge from the burning labyrinth and into the open air just as a fire engine wails on to the scene. I spot Dad and a bunch of other firefighters pouring out, heading for the blazing maze. He doesn't see me, probably because we're not sticking around. We don't wait to see what's become of the hound.

Instead, we run as though our lives depend on it — which, for a few minutes there, they did.

★

'You have to tell your dads,' Roo urges. 'This is all getting too big for us now.'

I shake my head.

'No way, not after what happened today. If they realize that the animal that ruined the fete has been living under the same roof as them for the last few weeks, they'll *lose* it.'

We're back in the tree house. The fete was quickly evacuated. Nobody had been able to identify the bizarre ball of fire that set everything ablaze, which was a relief. But there was no mention of any charred remains at the centre of the maze, which is why we're not celebrating the Grendilock's downfall just yet. For all we know, it's still out there somewhere.

'So what are you going to do?' asks Roo.

I shrug and look down at Cadno, who's asleep in my arms. He's another reason we're not celebrating. He was sluggish the whole way home and now all he wants to do is sleep, although he does jerk away if anyone goes near his left paw. There's a lump halfway down his front leg, and I can see a red gash at the top of it, the fur around it knotted with blood.

A bite.

'I don't know,' I admit. 'You guys shouldn't have come after me. You could have been really hurt.'

Lippy rolls her eyes. 'Charlie, shush.'

Roo nods. 'Yeah. As if we were going to leave you to get mauled by that . . . that *thing*. What are best friends for, eh?'

I smile feebly. 'Well, thank you. You saved our lives.'

We lapse into silence. And, even though I'm grateful to them, despair tugs at me. I'm supposed to be keeping Cadno safe, and I'm not doing a very good job of it.

I was just starting to feel good about myself. My inner fire was just beginning to grow. I even stood up to Will and Zack. But who am I kidding? I can't do this. Cadno is hurt. And I would have lost him to the Grendilock today if Lippy and Roo hadn't arrived.

I still need them to rescue me. The thought sits

there, at the front of my mind. I still can't save myself.
Their fire feeds mine. It can't blaze by itself just yet.

'Do you think he's OK?' asks Roo.

'I hope so,' I say, blinking back the pressure that's
building behind my eyes. 'I'll try him with some
food soon, to get his strength up. How about your
favourite, eh? D'you fancy some corned beef, Cadno?'

The cub is either so deeply asleep that he doesn't
hear me, or he's deliberately not responding.
Whichever it is, his reaction is uncharacteristic.

'I'm going to keep a close eye on him,' I declare,
trying to sound more confident than I feel.

We look down at the firecub cradled in my arms.
His fur seems dull, lacklustre. A heaviness settles over
my heart.

He's not right. He's really not right.

Chapter 20

'How's my little firefluff doing today?' Lippy coos. She beckons Cadno into her arms, but he barely acknowledges her. Instead, he tucks himself up against me.

'He's worse,' I say. I stayed by Cadno's side the whole night, although he barely stirred. He wasn't interested in his water, and his nose didn't twitch when I brought up a plate of corned beef. He didn't even flinch when my dads came up to check on me. He just stayed under the blanket while I told them I had no idea what happened at the fete. 'I need to clean his cut, but he won't let me get near it.'

The wound has stopped bleeding, but his leg looks swollen and painful.

Afternoon is passing into evening, and we're in the tree house. Roo sits down on a beanbag, his face puckered with concern. 'What do you think we should do?'

They must be able to sense how lost I feel because Lippy scoots closer to me.

'Don't worry, Charlie,' she says. 'Maybe Teg will come back soon. He'll know what to do.'

'Maybe he'll be able to do some magic to help him heal,' says Roo. 'Like a witch doctor!'

'Teg just works in the royal kitchens. I don't think he can do magic . . .'

I freeze, realization hitting me in the face like a sledgehammer.

'That's it,' I say. 'That's it! Roo, you're brilliant!'

'Eh?' Roo frowns.

'Witch doctor!' I exclaim. 'Why didn't I think of this sooner? Lippy, your mum's a doctor!'

'No, she's not, she's a vet –' Lippy begins, but then her mouth drops open. 'You're right! My mother's a vet! Roo, you're a genius!'

'I-I am? Er, I mean, yeah, I am!' He puffs his chest out. 'I'm a genius! That was totally my idea!'

I laugh and hug my friends, holding Cadno slightly apart so that he doesn't get squished. But then Lippy pulls away, her expression serious.

'Charlie, are you sure about this? I don't think my mum has ever treated a fox before, especially not a *magical* fox.'

'She's our only hope!' I urge. 'We have to take Cadno to her so she can help him get better.'

Lippy takes a deep breath. 'You're right. But it's Sunday, so the surgery is closed. I'll phone her and ask her to meet us there.'

I look down at Cadno as Lippy pulls out her phone and starts talking to her mum. He blinks drowsily up at me.

'Just a bit longer,' I say to him. 'We'll get you help in no time.'

We take it in turns carrying Cadno as we head across town. Up until today, he's eaten pretty much everything I've put in front of him, so just a few minutes of lugging his portly body around is enough to deaden my arms.

By the time we reach Pet Hospital, we're all panting, but Stella's car is parked outside and, while my arms ache, my heart fills with light.

'Mum must be inside already,' says Lippy, and she glances at me. 'Are you ready, Charlie?'

'I'm ready,' I reply.

Then, as a single unit, we cross the road.

The reception area is dim. Stella bursts out of one of the appointment rooms to the left as we enter.

'Lippy, love, what's all this about?' she asks. 'Have you been rescuing animals again? If this is like the time you brought in that stray cat −'

She pauses when she sees the three of us standing

there. Her gaze settles on Cadno, curled up in my arms, and she looks alarmed.

'You *have* been rescuing animals again. But a fox? Lippy, this is a bit extreme, even for you,' she says. 'That's a wild animal. He could have all manner of –'

'He's not wild,' I blurt.

Stella stops short. 'What do you mean?'

'He's not wild,' I repeat. 'I mean, his *behaviour* can sometimes be wild, but he's actually a domestic fox. His name is Cadno, and he needs your help, Mrs Tarquin.'

Stella looks at her daughter. 'Lippy, can you please explain what's going on here?'

Lippy hesitates. 'I, er . . .'

'He's not a normal fox,' I say. 'He's a firefox.'

And, just like that, the words are out. Somebody else is in on *our* secret. There's no going back now.

Stella rolls her eyes. 'All right, somebody better tell me what's really happening –'

'He's telling the truth, Mum,' says Lippy. Her face is solemn.

'Look, I can show you,' I say, 'but first we need you to promise that you won't freak out.'

Stella's laughter rumbles across the room. 'That's not really the sort of thing you should say to instil confidence in a grown-up, you know!'

'I know, but it's all I've got.'

Stella takes a few seconds to consider before nodding.

I cautiously put Cadno down on the laminate flooring and step away from him. He looks up at me with his enormous eyes and lets out a whimper. He just wants to be held close. But Stella needs to believe us, and then she'll help him.

She watches Cadno carefully. At first, he just looks like an ordinary fox cub, but, as his whine builds, his fur takes on that familiar glow. His warm yellow light splashes against the wall, and I see Stella's expression go from curious to bewildered.

'What on earth . . .' she mutters, and then Cadno's fur begins to ripple with fire. Stella's mouth opens in panic, but, before she can move, Cadno erupts into

a flickering blaze. I instantly kneel down, as close
to the heat as my body will let me, and whisper
soothingly to him.

'*Shh*, Cadno,' I say. 'It's OK, boy. I'm here now.
I'm not leaving you. This nice lady is going to help
you, I promise.'

It takes a minute, but at last Cadno's flames shrink
back into his fur before disappearing altogether.

I open up my arms and he scurries into them, his coat still very warm. I stroke him from his ears to his tail, the way he likes.

I stand up again. Stella is staring at him, her eyes wide with astonishment.

'I've never seen anything like it,' she says finally.

'It doesn't hurt him or anything,' I say quickly. 'It's part of him. It's how he expresses himself. When he's hurt, angry, scared, sad . . . His fire is a bit like his soul, I think.'

'I don't understand.'

'You don't have to. Please, just help him. He's hurt,' I plead.

Stella looks from Cadno to us, and then back again. Finally, her attention settles on him. The fear leaves her face, replaced instead by an intense wonderment. But then, as soon as it appears, it vanishes and she glares at us.

'What on earth have you lot got yourselves into?' she hisses. 'Where did you get this animal from? Where have you been keeping him?'

'Please, Mrs Tarquin, there's no time,' I reply. 'I'll tell you everything once you've had a look at him.'

Stella's stony expression doesn't shift. 'Do your dads know about this?' I shake my head, and Stella takes a deep breath.

'Of course I'll help him, the poor thing, but then you're telling me more about what he is, where he came from and how he ended up in your hands. And then we're going to tell your dads.'

I open my mouth to argue, but close it when I realize there's no point. I just need Cadno to be OK. If that means telling the grown-ups about him, then so be it.

Lippy runs forward and throws her arms round her mother. 'Thank you so much, Mum!'

'Thank you, Mrs Tarquin,' I breathe.

'I'm a vet, Charlie,' she says. 'This is what I do. I can't bear to see an animal hurt. And call me Stella. Now bring him in here.'

I scoop Cadno up, careful not to jolt his injured paw, and carry him through to the appointment room. I set him down on the examination table but keep my hands on him at all times, ruffling him gently between the ears.

'That . . . fantastic light display,' says Stella as she pulls on some gloves, 'will he do it again if I touch him?'

I shake my head. 'I don't think so. He's quite calm. Just go slowly.'

I turn my attention to the firecub. 'You have to let her get close to you. She won't hurt you, I promise. She's going to help you.'

Cadno blinks up at me and then turns back to Stella.

'Go ahead,' I say.

Stella reaches out, cautiously at first, but then her fingers brush the fluffy fur on the top of his head, and she lets out a delighted gasp.

'Oh my goodness!' she gasps, tears glistening in her eyes. She lowers her hand on to Cadno's head, and he leans into her touch. 'He is wonderful! He's so warm!'

'He is,' I agree, but then I clear my throat. 'Mrs Tarquin . . .'

'Stella,' she corrects me. 'Now tell me — what's wrong?'

'It's his paw. He can't put any weight on it, and he won't eat or drink anything either.'

Stella leans in close to examine his leg. It's even more swollen than it was yesterday. I try to read her expression, but it betrays nothing. She's completely focused.

'What happened to him?'

'He was . . . bitten.'

'By what?'

I don't answer.

'What on earth have you lot got yourselves into?' Stella mutters under her breath again, and then she sighs. 'I'm going to need to clean it, then possibly give him some stitches. You'll have to step outside, but don't worry: he's in safe hands with me.'

Panic rises in me. 'Is he going to be OK?'

Stella hurries round the table to shepherd us out. 'Yes. But I really need to get started.'

She ushers us into the waiting room. I'm trying to peer past her, to get one last look at my newest best friend –

'It won't take long,' says Stella.

She gives me a sympathetic glance, and then slams the door shut.

We wait for what feels like hours. I keep imagining Cadno in that cold, whitewashed room, lying under the glare of the veterinary light. It takes so much willpower to stop myself from bursting through the door and snatching him up.

But finally, after about thirty minutes, the door opens, and Stella steps out. The three of us jump to our feet.

'Is he OK?' I exclaim.

Stella smiles. 'He's going to be fine.'

I start to cheer, but then the air is knocked out of me by my two friends embracing me from both sides.

I don't think I've ever felt such happiness.

'The bite wasn't as bad as it looked. He didn't need stitches, thankfully. I've given it a good clean and bandaged it up. It should mend by itself, as long as he doesn't move about too much – or burn the strapping off. He'll need to stay calm and relaxed so that he has time to heal.'

Lippy, Roo and I start celebrating again, parading round the waiting room with our arms in the air.

'Can we go in to see him?' I ask, breaking off from my friends.

Stella nods and stands aside. I hurry past her, and there he is, sitting handsomely on the examination table with a white bandage round his left leg. His tail starts to swish frantically when he sees me. We've only been apart for half an hour, but he smothers me with kisses when I pull him close.

'I missed you, little dynamite.'

'Charlie,' says Stella from the doorway. 'Remember what I said about keeping him calm?'

'Oh yeah.' I step back and run my hands from the

top of Cadno's head to the bottom of his spine. He leans into every stroke, his eyes closing in bliss.

'I've given him an anti-inflammatory tablet,' says Stella. 'It will help with the pain and the swelling. I'm going to give you a box of them to take with you. Just hide one in his food at mealtimes. He should regain his appetite once the tablets kick in.'

I look at Stella, my gratitude suddenly so overwhelming that I have to stop tears from falling. I was so scared that Cadno was seriously hurt, that this was all my fault.

'Thank you so much for helping him, Stella,' I say. 'I don't know how to repay you.'

'You can repay me by telling me exactly what's going on,' she replies. 'And then by telling your dads.'

I falter. I can't get out of this one. She's helped us enormously . . .

I open my mouth to speak, but at that very moment my phone vibrates in my pocket. I pull it out and glance at the screen.

It's a message from Dad.

Don't come home. There's something in the house. Go to Lippy's or Roo's. Phone the police.

'Oh no,' I say under my breath.

'Charlie, what's wrong?' I hear Lippy ask. I don't look up. I'm still staring at those words.

'My dads,' I whisper, my mind numb. 'They're in trouble. I have to go.'

Before anybody can reply, I grab Cadno and bolt for the door.

'Charlie, wait!'

'Can't!' I call back. 'I have to get to them!'

There's no point calling the police – they wouldn't believe me anyway. As I burst out into the night, I can't help but wonder if the Grendilock has got the better of me at last.

Chapter 21

Our house is in darkness. The front door is wide open.

Fear pulses through my veins. Fear for my dads. Fear of what is waiting for me inside. I tried calling both their phones as I darted home, but neither answered.

With Cadno in my arms, I race up to the front door – and then freeze. The darkness within feels alive. I've never been afraid of the dark, or afraid of our house, and yet here I am: too scared to step inside.

I take a deep breath. I have to do this. Cadno glances

up at me and licks my chin, like he's trying to give me a little bit of his fire. I step into the house, Cadno held against my chest. I should leave him outside, just in case something in there sets him off. But I need him. The blackness gobbles us up.

'D-Dad? Pa?' I call, wrinkling my nose. A foul stench rakes the back of my throat. It smells of things that are rotting in the mud. I've smelled it before – in the outbuilding of the veterinary surgery.

The Grendilock has been here.

And it's clear from the silence that slithers towards me from all corners of the house that it isn't here any longer. But neither are my dads. Did they escape? Maybe they're hiding somewhere, like the tree house.

I'm about to make my way to the back door when I almost slip on something on the floor. I pick it up – it's my red-and-navy baseball cap. The one I lost when the Grendilock was chasing us. Well, that explains how it traced me to our house. It must have picked it up and used it to track –

Cadno barks. The silence has been so absolute that the sound catches me off guard.

'What is it, boy?'

He's heating up, his fur beginning to shimmer with threads of hot wire. I put him down and watch as he circles round to face the hallway wall. A low, foreboding growl works its way up from his belly, and then his flames emerge. Yellow light splashes against the wall, and I let out a gasp.

There's a message slashed into the wallpaper. It looks as though it was done with a knife – or talons.

WE AWAIT YOU AT THE CASTLE.
BRING HIM.

It comes in many forms, Teg said back when all of this started. It looks like the Grendilock finally abandoned its hound disguise in order to write this message. Perhaps it changed form before – to open the gate to the outbuilding at the vet's, I realize.

It doesn't take a genius to figure out who 'him' is. The Grendilock wants Cadno. But it's the very first word that chills me to my core.

We.

That must mean my dads. It's taken them as hostages. One swift trade – Cadno in exchange for my parents.

I suddenly feel as though my whole world has fallen apart.

There's no running away from this. I have to go up to the castle. My dads wanted me to phone the police, but what would I tell them? *Please help, officer – a monster kidnapped my dads!* Yeah, right.

No. This is up to me.

I'm turning back to the door when I spot something else on the ground. Two somethings, actually.

The first is a smooth, round amber stone with a swirl painted on it. Teg's sealstone. The Grendilock used it to get into our world, and then dropped it when it came to my house in search of Cadno.

I don't have time to ponder what this means for Teg, though, because it's the other something that really puzzles me: a denim handbag.

And that's when it all falls into place. Something Teg said replays in my mind: *It can take many forms, its favourite being the hound. But they're all monstrous in their own way.*

Oh yes, the Grendilock has found us. But it would seem that it's been under our noses for a while, covering its tracks with pink slip-on shoes, and its sickening smell with a spritz of sugary perfume.

'Tanya Cleck,' I whisper.

I can't waste any more time, but then an ear-splitting sound shatters the silence of the house. It's the Heat Hunter 3000, finally picking up on the blaze that is flowering from Cadno's fur.

'Come on, boy,' I say. 'Let's go and get our family.'

We're just running up the garden path, and on to the street, when a pair of familiar figures come rushing towards us.

'What are you two doing here?' I cry, a mixture of

relief and annoyance bubbling in my stomach.

Lippy and Roo skid to a standstill next to me, both of them panting. Cadno's painkiller tablet must have kicked in, because he's leaping round their ankles. His bandage has been burned off already, I notice.

'We followed you! Did you honestly think we were going to leave you to tackle this alone?' asks Lippy.

'It's going to be really dangerous,' I point out.

'Hey, we've been there for every other dangerous situation over the last couple of weeks,' says Roo. 'Why stop now?'

'All right, suit yourselves,' I sigh, secretly feeling thankful.

'What happened in there?' asks Roo, glancing at the open front door. 'What's that *noise*?'

'That's the fire alarm. Cadno set it off. We haven't got much time. Remember Tanya Cleck?'

My friends nod.

'Well, she's actually been the Grendilock all this time, and now it looks like she's kidnapped my dads so that she can get to Cadno. Come on. We really have to go.'

Lippy gawps. 'I *knew* there was something off about her! But wait . . . where are we going?'

'Back to where this all began,' I reply, as I start marching down the street. 'Don't worry, I'll explain everything. The Grendilock has my parents and, if we're going to get them back, we need your little sister's hamster.'

We go straight to Lippy's house. Stella's car isn't there. Lippy said she and Roo had to run off to catch up with me, but that her mum was shouting after them the whole time. She must be out looking for us.

'Wait here,' Lippy says, and then vanishes round the back of the house. Roo, Cadno and I wait for a few anxious minutes before Lippy reappears with a transparent ball clasped in her hands. Inside is a hamster with fat cheeks.

'Here he is,' she says.

'Yo, Dorito,' says Roo. Dorito licks his tiny paws and swipes at his ears.

'Please tell me what you're going to do with him,' Lippy pleads. 'He's a good hamster.'

'Dorito isn't going to get hurt,' I promise. 'In fact, he's going to be a hero.'

When my friends frown at me, I go on. 'When I met Teg, he told me about Fargone, how it's home to tons of crazy stuff, like these giant emperor rats that can eat you for lunch. And, when I started thinking about it, it all adds up. In the outbuilding at the vet's, the Grendilock went to the wrong cage. It didn't find Cadno, it found Tinkles the gerbil – and freaked out. And then, at the fete, Tanya freaked out again when we started talking about rats –'

'It's scared of rodents,' Lippy says, a smile working its way on to her face. 'Because, in Fargone, the rodents are bigger than it is.'

'Exactly,' I grin. 'And we're going to turn Dorito into our very own giant emperor rat.'

We race through town until we reach the castle

hill, following the zigzag path as best we can in the darkness. I can hear Dorito scratching in his ball as the castle's outer walls rise before us. We hurry across the drawbridge and under the portcullis, the moon our only source of light.

We pick our way across the grounds that surround the towers until we reach the clearing on the other side, dappled with silver moonlight. I press myself against the curved wall of the north-west tower, signalling for Lippy and Roo to do the same, and then I peer round it.

There they are. My dads, near the curtain of ivy against the far wall. They're tied back-to-back with rope, their mouths taped, their faces etched with fear – but they're OK. I almost cry out with relief.

But I don't. Because they're not alone. Walking towards the curtain of ivy is somebody familiar. Blonde beehive hair and pink fluffy jacket.

It's Tanya Cleck, holding a length of rope that leads back to my dads. She comes to a stop in front of the open gateway, the darkness from beyond deeper somehow than the surrounding night. She stands there for several minutes, staring – as though she's waiting for something. Or someone.

Suddenly she lifts her head and extends her neck. And I can't see her face, but I can tell that she's sniffing the air. A tendril of fear creeps up my spine. Then she speaks and, though her tone is low, her words fill the entire clearing.

'I knew that you would come.'

Chapter 22

Lippy and Roo go rigid. Cadno begins to shimmer in my arms. I shoot my friends an urgent glance before stepping out into the open.

'Give me my dads back,' I say. My voice sounds so small compared to hers.

My dads spot me from the other side of the clearing. They squirm against their bindings, their mouths sealed and their cheeks streaked with dirt. They look petrified, confused – but, more than that, angry. I know if I were to remove their gags, they'd

243

be telling me to run for it.

Tanya stays facing the ivy, her shoulders starting to shake. She's laughing. The sound of it fills the air, and it's so devoid of joy that it makes me feel empty inside.

'How charming,' she says. 'Not even a please. Do they not teach the children in this world any manners? The court would have a royal fit.'

A vile odour crawls up my nostrils. The smell of rot – the very same that I smelled back at my house.

Tanya turns round, and this time I can't fight back a strangled cry.

Her eyes aren't human any more. They are beady and black. Insectile. They belong to something that crawls across the forest floor, something that feasts on dead, decaying flesh. She isn't human; she's a monster. Her cheeks are pocked with burn marks and blisters – from the fire in the maze, I imagine.

The more I think about it, the more it makes sense. The strange way she talked. The way she wore her shoes on the wrong feet. The way her face was covered in paint instead of make-up – and then how she got better at it the next time I saw her. The Grendilock was *learning* how to be a human being from scratch, and in the worst possible way – by looking at old fashion magazines, ones that made it think that women had to wear pink and slather on lots of make-up. That people *had* to be a certain way and fit into a certain box.

Well, it couldn't be more wrong. Nobody has to fit into a box – my family is proof of that.

I feel so small in front of Tanya now. But the fire that drove me here is still smouldering inside. Tanya tilts her head at me. She doesn't blink. Her gaze falls on Cadno, who stands next to me, snarling, his heat so intense that I can only just bear to be near him.

Something flashes out from Tanya's mouth, snake-like. It's her tongue. She licks the air, gooey saliva dripping down her chin. It's as if she can *taste* Cadno on the night breeze.

'Despite your lack of etiquette, I am willing to bargain,' says Tanya, her tongue slithering back into her mouth. 'I have what is yours, and you have what is mine. Give me the firefox, and you can have your guardians. It is a fair exchange. The choice is yours.'

I look over at my dads. They stare at me, their eyes tearful. Then I glance down at Cadno. He's fired up, his fur flickering dangerously. He's ready to stand his ground. Well, so am I.

I don't have to choose between them. That's what the Grendilock wants me to do, but it's not what *I'm* here to do. I'm tired of being pushed around, monster or no monster.

I spare a quick sideways glance at Lippy and Roo. They're gawping at me from the shadows. I give them the tiniest shake of my head. Not yet. They need to stick to the plan, no matter what. They need to wait for the signal.

'You don't have to do this,' I plead. 'Please just give me my dads back.'

'If only it were that simple, you rotten little cockroach.' She sighs. 'Do you have any idea of the ransom that King Aran is offering in exchange for the return of the last firefox? More gold than I could spend in a lifetime.'

'But what will he do with him?'

'Oh, I do not know – parade him in front of his royal subjects?' Tanya cackles. 'Teach the little rat some fancy tricks? Before you know it, he will be walking on his hind legs, balancing turnips on his head and putting on firework displays. And then, when he is too old to perform, he will be used as a nice footrest. Or, better still, turned into a cloak. I do not particularly care, so long as I get my reward.'

I imagine Cadno standing on his hind legs while around him the court of Fargone laughs and jeers. My skin crawls with revulsion. Cadno isn't some circus act for people's entertainment. He's a living, breathing animal. He needs to be free. He needs open air and a fresh breeze and a world to explore. He needs love.

He needs *me*, just like I need him.

'Now stop all this nonsense,' Tanya orders, her slimy tongue forking out again. 'Getting my hands on that wretched beast has taken far too long already. Tracking you down was easy enough. It was like you *wanted* me to find you. But you were never alone. Always surrounded by people. And, when I did get you on your own, you slipped through my fingers. But then you led me straight to that useless social worker, and I was able to mimic her pathetic husk of a body. I knew you had the beast, but I could not smell it at your dwelling, so I could not be sure where you were hiding it.'

I think back to Tanya's visit. That was why Cadno had been hiding in the fresh towels basket – to mask his scent. And the day before that – when Pam called in – I *did* see the hound's scarlet eyes in the bushes. It was watching us. I wonder what really happened to Pam, and a chill passes over me.

'But I tire of the pretence now. You have

delayed me long enough. Hand over the fox,' Tanya commands, her eyes glinting dangerously, 'or I shall take it from you – and it will not be painless, boy. I may even decide to bear your guardians back to Fargone with me, too. Mayhap the king will reward me even more handsomely if I bring him a new pair of servants as well.'

'You can't have him,' I say, but my voice is small. I clear my throat and speak again, louder this time: 'You can't have him! And you can't have my dads either!'

At that, Tanya smiles.

'What a surprise,' she says, her lips peeling back from her teeth in the most repulsive way. 'Quiet little Charlie is fighting back. Such a shame. I had hoped to leave you to live out your days in the knowledge that you failed to rescue both your *pest* and your guardians. But alas, you give me no choice but to destroy you.'

As Tanya speaks, her body starts to shudder and expand, like a balloon being pumped up.

'I will say,' she goes on, her voice deepening as her frame bulges and pops, 'I am glad to finally shed this

wretched form. You humans are so fragile, so pitiful, so *weak*.'

I watch in horror as Tanya's human clothes burst into tatters and flutter to the ground. Her entire body is stretching, her limbs elongating until her sinewy arms almost drag along the floor. Her skin is grey and mottled and has a sickly sheen to it, like a dead fish. Thin, filthy straggles of black hair grow in patches from her arms and scalp. Her eyes bulge in her head, as though they're too big for her skull, and her teeth jut from her gums like shards of broken glass. Her whole face seems to twist out of shape, her mouth protruding – or her lips shrinking away from her gums – as if they can't contain all of the teeth inside.

It can take many forms, Teg had said. The hound was one. Tanya was another. Now I'm seeing the Grendilock in its truest form. And it's worse than anything I have ever imagined. I want to close my eyes. I want to turn round and run away.

But I can't. I can only watch as Tanya Cleck

vanishes and is replaced instead by this beetle-eyed, wolfish nightmare. The Grendilock. The rotten smell becomes so strong I feel as though I'm going to be violently sick.

Cadno snarls furiously.

'Silence!' the Grendilock snaps, and that's when I realize that not only does it not *look* human any more – it *doesn't sound* human either, its voice guttural and rasping.

It sinks down on to all fours, and still it's bigger than a horse. It shifts its weight back on to its hind legs, spittle glistening on its teeth as it prepares to launch itself across the open space.

Now. It needs to happen now.

'Wait,' I say, and the Grendilock pauses. It fixes me with its cold, joyless glare.

'What is it, boy?'

'Before, you asked me if I have any pets,' I say. 'Do you remember? At the fete? And I told you I didn't? Well, I was lying.'

'I know you were lying!' the creature barks,

saliva flying from its mouth. 'Stop wasting my time –'

'I wasn't lying about Cadno,' I say quickly. 'I mean, I was, but I was lying about something else, too. I *do* have a pet.'

The Grendilock's eyes twitch uncertainly.

'In fact, I brought him here with me today,' I say, and I cast Lippy and Roo a fleeting glance. Lippy has already got Dorito in her hands, and Roo is pointing his phone at her. They're ready.

'He's a giant emperor rat,' I say. 'His name is Dorito.'

The Grendilock flinches. 'An . . . e-emperor rat?'

'Oh, didn't you know we have those here, too? In fact, I think they're even bigger than the ones in Fargone. Humungous, actually. Twice as big as you are.'

'You lie,' the Grendilock snarls.

'I don't,' I say, and then I glance in Lippy and Roo's direction. 'Oh look, here he comes now. He seems angry. Hey, Dorito!'

As I speak, Roo presses the torch on his phone, and a blinding white light bursts from the back, splashing all over the walls behind me – and casting the monstrous black shadow of an emperor rat, swiping the air with its gargantuan claws.

The Grendilock lets out a terrified scream and cowers back towards the gateway. Its eyes are wide and, while I didn't think it possible for such a frightening beast to seem vulnerable, it does – it looks like it wants to run away.

And then it does exactly that. The emperor rat takes a single step forward, its shadow growing even larger, and that's enough to finish the Grendilock off. It turns and dives through the curtain of ivy, into the gateway and out of sight, its shriek fading as it goes.

We wait a few seconds and then I let out a delighted whoop.

'It worked! It really worked!'

Lippy and Roo rush forward and flatten me in a hug, although Lippy is careful not to squash little Dorito. Cadno tries to lick all three of our faces at once.

'It's OK, boy,' I laugh, 'I've got you. You're not going anywhere!'

I hear muffled cries behind me and turn to see my dads struggling against their bindings.

'Hold on!' I call, setting Cadno down. I run over to untie them, but instead of joy I see terror in their eyes. They're looking at something behind me, their cheeks flushed as they try to scream. Behind me is the gateway.

A putrid smell overwhelms me. I feel a hot, sickening puff of air against the nape of my neck, and I turn slowly.

The head of the Grendilock is peering back through the curtain of ivy. I can see myself reflected in the empty blackness of its insect eyes.

I look afraid.

Chapter 23

The Grendilock glares over my shoulder, taking in the scene beyond me. I turn, too, and see Lippy and Roo standing, frozen in terror on the other side of the clearing. Dorito is back in his ball now, looking particularly tiny and squishable.

I return my attention to the Grendilock. It flashes its pointed teeth. 'You deceived me, boy.'

'I-I . . .' I stammer, but the Grendilock doesn't waste another second. It crashes back through the curtain of ivy and suddenly it's on top of me, pinning me to the ground with its muscular arms. Long black hairs as thick as spider legs brush my face, and my stomach churns.

It roars in my face, spittle flecking my cheeks. I try to shrink away, but there's no escape. I close my eyes. This is it. The end.

A familiar yap cuts through the night beyond the Grendilock's hulking form. The monster turns its head, and I peer past it.

Cadno is standing in the middle of the clearing, his stance proud. He flares into a ferocious ball of fire. The Grendilock instantly forgets me, a furious roar tearing from its throat.

'Get over here, you filthy furball!'

Cadno gives the Grendilock a mocking bark. The Grendilock's entire body judders with rage, and then it rampages across the space with outstretched arms. Cadno bolts forward, through the monster's legs, just like he did with Roo and the football, and vanishes through the archway in the wall that leads into the north-west tower.

The Grendilock lets out an incensed roar and twists round. It hurtles past me and disappears after Cadno, the ground shuddering as it thunders by.

I scramble to my feet, determined to rescue Cadno. I glance desperately at my dads. They look petrified, but they're going to be safer tied up here for now than anywhere else.

'Stay with them!' I yell to Lippy and Roo. 'But don't untie them until I get back. I don't want them to follow me and get hurt.'

'But, Charlie –' Roo starts.

I'm already running across the clearing. 'Please just do it!' I cry, and then the sky lights up above me. I hear a terrifying roar.

I crane my neck, my gaze travelling up the north-west tower. There, at the very top, spouting flames like a newly erupting volcano, is

Cadno. An enormous shape
appears beyond him, and
I shout out in warning,
but they're too far away.
I need to get closer if
I'm going to stand any
chance of helping him.

I duck through the archway and take the spiral staircase that leads to the top of the tower. The steps are steep and narrow. They go on and on, until finally I see a sliver of night above me. The stairway opens up on to a familiar circular roof ringed with jagged battlements. I peer over the lip of the top stair, not wanting to give myself away completely. All I have is the element of surprise.

The Grendilock stands at the centre of the terrace, its back turned to me. I hadn't noticed before, but it has a very long, sinewy tail tipped with a barb of coarse black hair that slashes back and forth.

Cadno stands at the edge of the terrace, his flames swirling round him in a mighty storm. I can feel the heat from where I crouch. The Grendilock obviously has a high resistance because it takes a step closer. Beyond Cadno is the long drop down to the central courtyard fenced in by the four towers.

'Come now, little imp,' it says. 'Let us get you back to Fargone. I am going to persuade the king to skin you alive for all the trouble you have caused me.'

It doesn't know I'm here. That has to count for something. I can stop this revolting monstrosity. I just have to wait for the right moment. The Grendilock takes another step closer to Cadno.

Now!

I leap forward with my arms outstretched, a triumphant scream building in my throat. Cadno spots me and dives out of the way just as my hands ram against the Grendilock's back.

The Grendilock, caught unawares, staggers forward. Its momentum carries it directly over the edge of the tower and, with a final roar of fury, it disappears into the darkness.

Or at least I think it does. I'm just turning to hug Cadno when something snakes round my ankle and tugs me through the air. A clawed hand. Suddenly I'm hurtling towards the edge of the tower, a petrified cry gurgling in my throat.

I slip over the edge, my hands struggling for purchase. My fingers find a crevice and I cling on, suspended thirty metres above the central courtyard below.

My heart pounds in my throat; my blood roars in my ears. My ankle feels as though it's about to break, most of the Grendilock's immense weight hanging from it as its back legs scrabble to get a grip on the tower wall. Its wicked laugh rises up to me.

'If I cannot get the cub, then neither shall you!'

So this is it. I can only hold on for a few seconds longer – my fingers are slipping. It's going to take me down with it.

Cadno appears above me, his fire burning brightly. He lets out a wolf-like howl that drowns out the dreadful laugh of the Grendilock, and, as I desperately try to heave myself back over the edge of the platform, my knuckles nudge something hard.

My hand closes round it, and I realize what it is. It's a rock from the crumbled turret that I hid my painted pebble inside. It feels like so long ago now. I heave it towards me, tightening my grip on the crevice with my other hand so that I don't fall yet.

I remember the design I painted on to my pebble. Fire. I didn't even know about Cadno when I painted it. I was small and afraid, but now the universe has brought me back to its hiding place. And this time my inner fire is finally ablaze.

'You cannot hold on much longer, boy!' shouts the Grendilock. 'Bid farewell to your guardians!'

And that's all it takes. That single word.

'THEY'RE NOT MY GUARDIANS!' I roar, wrenching the rock free and hurling it downwards with all my might.

The Grendilock looks up at the very last second, its gaze filling with terrible realization, and then the rock hits it squarely between the eyes. It winces stupidly, and I can see from the way its body stiffens that it's stunned. Its grip on my ankle loosens, and it falls.

I close my eyes just as a sickening *crunch* echoes up through the night.

I clamber back over the edge of the turret and roll on to my back.

'They're my *dads*,' I mutter, my chest heaving with exhaustion.

A fireball collides with me. It bombards me with kisses, its chubby little body trembling with joy. I can feel heat through my clothes, cooling by the second as he tries not to burn me.

'I've got you, Cadno,' I say, smiling up at the stars. 'I've got you.'

Chapter 24

I dread reaching the bottom of the tower and seeing the remains of the Grendilock, but, by the time I get there and glance into the central courtyard, the Grendilock seems to have turned to something like charcoal and is crumbling away. The night is quiet again, peaceful even.

I pick Cadno up and we make our way through the archway and into the clearing, where Lippy and Roo sit crouched next to Dad and Pa against the far wall, their faces knitted in concentration as they struggle to loosen the knots that bind them together.

'Hold the torch still, Roo, I can't see what I'm doing.'

'Well, you keep moving all the time!'

'Charlie!' cries Dad, his mouth ungagged.

Their faces light up when they spot me, but then they start scanning the shadows.

'Don't worry,' I say. 'It's gone.'

And I can't quite believe it myself. The Grendilock is gone. Because of *me*.

'Charlie!'

Lippy and Roo envelop me in a bone-crushing hug. Cadno is caught in the middle – not that he seems to mind. He laps up all the love, his tail swishing happily.

'What happened?' demands Lippy.

'Is it *gone* gone?' asks Roo.

'Oh, it's very, *very* gone,' I assure them. 'I'll tell you the whole story. But first . . .'

I break off and make my way over to my dads. I finish untying them and we collapse to the ground in

what might be the tightest hug I've ever experienced.
But it's also the loveliest.

It's over as soon as it started. Suddenly I'm on my
feet and being held at arm's length by Pa, who studies
me closely, concern and anger etched on his face.

Uh-oh.

'What on *earth* were you thinking?' he exclaims.
'G-going after that . . . that *thing* like you did? You
should have gone to the police, like we told you to!
You could have been killed, Charlie.' His eyes become
misty. 'All of you, you could have been killed!'

267

'I know, I know,' I say. 'But we weren't! And now we're all alive and the Grendilock is gone!'

'W-what happened to Tanya? What was that . . . *thing* that she turned into?' Dad blurts. 'Charlie, you've got some serious explaining to do.'

At the mention of Tanya, Lippy and Roo actually laugh. I find myself smiling, too.

'And I will; I'll explain everything,' I promise. 'No more secrets. But first there's somebody I'd like you to meet.'

I open up my arms slightly. Cadno peeps out from the crook of my elbow and blinks up at them.

'Cadno, meet my dads,' I say. 'Dads, meet Cadno. He's actually been living with us for a couple of weeks now. And I don't know if you noticed earlier, but he's not your average fox. He's actually a firefox. The last firefox, as a matter of fact.'

Pa takes two steps back. 'I'm dreaming.'

Dad stares at Cadno, wide-eyed. 'Charlie, you are in *so* much trouble,' he says sternly, and my heart sinks. 'You know how I feel about open flames in the house! But then I do also feel quite strongly about adorable animals . . .'

Cadno's big eyes are luring him in. I can see it. He's only a few seconds away from becoming a puddle of fuzziness.

'Can we please get back on track?' Pa snaps. 'Charlie, you have so much explaining to do –'

He breaks off when Cadno raises his head and lifts a chunky paw, like he wants to shake hands.

'He wants to say hello,' I say to Pa. Fear flickers in my father's eyes.

'He won't hurt you,' I go on. 'He's harmless. Er, well, mostly harmless. His fire only comes out when he's angry, or scared, or hungry. Right now, he feels safe. Go on, touch him. He'll never hurt the ones that he loves.'

Dad prods Pa in the shoulder, and slowly Pa steps forward. He reaches out, his hand trembling ever so slightly, and strokes Cadno's forehead with the tip of his forefinger. His expression softens when he realizes that, despite the previous pyrotechnics, right now Cadno feels and looks just like a normal, fluffy, especially warm fox cub.

'My towels,' he says abruptly.

Dad frowns. 'What?'

'All those socks and towels that caught fire on the clothes line the other day,' says Pa, staring at Cadno. 'That was him!'

Oh no. Busted! 'Er, well . . . it was an accident —'

'You are in so, *so* much trouble, young man,' says Pa, but then he smiles. 'But that can wait until later. For now, I'm just glad you're all safe.'

He gives Cadno a nervous pat on the head, and then Dad joins in. I put him down, and Dad starts tousling him between the ears.

'Like this,' I say, running my hand from the top of his head to the bottom of his spine. 'It's his favourite.'

Dad smiles and follows suit, until Cadno extends his neck in glee. For the first time in what seems like forever, things feel right.

I take a deep breath. 'I have a lot to tell you, and you're probably not going to believe most of it.'

'Right now,' says Dad, unable to take his eyes off Cadno, 'I think I'll believe anything.'

'Well, that's good, but I don't think here is the best place to tell you everything.'

'Home,' says Dad. 'Let's start by going home.'

'Wait,' I say, remembering something. 'Not yet. There's something else I need to do.'

I reach into my pocket and pull out the sealstone that I picked up in the hallway. I can't leave the gateway open or something else might come through. But how on earth does it work . . . ?

A rustle of movement whispers from the ivy, and a familiar voice chimes through.

'Hey, that's mine!'

I look up, and there he is, in his furry brown coat, his big hazel eyes gleaming like lighthouse beacons.

'Teg!' I gasp. Cadno lets out a delighted bark and darts to Teg's feet.

Teg laughs as he lifts the cub into his arms. 'You've grown, little one!'

'Is he from school?' Dad whispers in my ear as Teg and Cadno dance around.

'Does he *look* like he goes to my school?'

Dad grimaces. 'Perhaps not.'

Teg comes to a standstill before me. 'Charlie,' he grins. 'Sorry I'm a tad late.'

'A tad?' I splutter. 'Where have you been? You said two days!'

A shadow passes over Teg's face. 'Yes, I did. And, believe me, I'm not late through choice. After I left you, the Grendilock caught up with me. It took my sealstone and left me to the mercy of the king. That's why I wasn't able to get back to you when I was supposed to. I'm sorry.'

Teg looks over his shoulder, at the ropes of ivy and the gateway to Fargone. 'Once again, I don't have much time. I escaped from my prison, but the king's men are after me. I don't want anything to follow me through the gateway –'

'Teg, the Grendilock was here,' I say. 'It's been hunting us this whole time.'

'What?' Teg tenses and glances into the shadows. 'Where is it now?'

'It's dead.'

He stares at me in shock. 'Dead? But how . . .' He trails off into an astounded silence and then shakes his head with a grin. 'It doesn't matter. What matters is that no harm has come to either of you. I asked you to look after Firetail because you were the only person around –'

'Yes, yes, all right,' I mutter.

Teg smiles. 'But I can see now that you were the best person for the job. Your heart is as bright as a firefox's. It was nothing more than embers when I first met you, but now the fire is burning strong.'

'I couldn't have done it without my friends,' I say, glancing over my shoulder at Lippy and Roo, who are both studying Teg curiously. 'They helped fight the Grendilock. Plus, they've helped me look after Cadno.'

'I even picked up poo from the garden,' says Roo, and I see Pa flinch.

'Then I am forever in your debt,' replies Teg, dipping into a bow. 'And I see you've renamed him!'

'Firetail just didn't sit right,' I say. Then I add meekly, 'I hope that's OK.'

Teg glances down at the cub in his arms and smiles. 'Cadno,' he says. 'It's perfect.'

Tears sting my eyes. 'He helped me more than I helped him, you know.'

Cadno lets out a little whine and wriggles in Teg's arms, as though he wants to get back to me.

'You helped each other, Charlie. But now I need you to make a decision.'

My heart thuds in my chest.

'The gateway between this world and mine must be destroyed to stop more of the king's hunters getting through. It must happen tonight. What you need to decide, Charlie, is whether Cadno stays in this world with you, or comes back to Fargone with me.'

Cadno and I lock gazes. I see myself reflected in

his enormous amber irises, but more than that – I see myself in this little ball of courage and fire. For the first time, I understand myself.

Cadno was running away from something when Teg brought him to me, just like I was. He had enemies, just like I did. We were both lost. We were both afraid. But we helped each other. Cadno has helped to fire up my soul. Teg is right. I *do* have fire in my heart, and it took falling in love with Cadno to make me realize that.

'Can I hold him?' I ask Teg, opening my arms.

Teg nods and passes the little pot-bellied fluff-ball over. Cadno butts his head against my cheek.

'Charlie, you should know that whatever decision you make tonight will be irreversible,' Teg warns me. 'If you choose to keep Cadno here with you, the legacy of the last firefox will be yours to protect. Forever. But, if you choose to let him come back with me to Fargone, you will never be able to see Cadno again.'

I glance over at my dads. Dad has his hand on Pa's

shoulder, and Pa is holding it fiercely.

'I know you don't understand yet,' I say to them, 'but I can't let him go back. Please. It's not safe for him there.'

I can see the conflict in their faces. Cadno is so alien to them. He still is to me sometimes, too. How can I expect them to take him in, just like that?

'It'll be just like having a puppy,' I try. 'Except a bit . . . sparky.'

There's a wobble in Dad's expression. He nudges Pa softly. 'We've always wanted a dog,' he says.

'Yes, a *dog*, Jack. Not . . . not this. What if he sets the house on fire?'

'Well, then it's a good thing I've got extinguishers in every room,' Dad says with a chuckle.

'Cadno would never do that,' I say, and he lets out a grunt of agreement. 'He thinks of my bedroom as his home. He would never do anything to damage that. Please?'

Dad pokes out his bottom lip in that coaxing sort

of way. Pa groans, spares Cadno a single glance – and that's it. He melts.

'Oh fine!' he huffs, and there's no mistaking the softness in his eyes. 'But I'm *not* cleaning up his poop, OK?'

My heart soars. 'Cadno, you're coming home!'

Cadno lets out a celebratory howl, and I laugh. Dad laughs, too, and even Pa can't help but smile. In just a few short seconds, we're all laughing. Lippy and Roo look as though they're about to burst with happiness.

'Are you sure that this is what you want to do, Charlie?' Teg asks me.

'More than I've ever been sure of anything.'

Teg nods. 'Then we must act. Now.'

We cross the clearing, the stars splayed above us. The ivy curtain rustles in the breeze, the darkness of the gateway whispering to us from beyond.

'As soon as I'm gone, you must destroy it,' Teg tells me. 'Do you understand?'

'How do I do that? With the sealstone?'

'The sealstone will only *close* the gateway. Anyone

with another sealstone could open it again. There is only one way to destroy a magical gateway,' Teg smiles, 'and that's with magical fire.'

I glance down at Cadno and nod.

'What's going to happen to you, Teg?' I ask, my heart suddenly filling with sadness. 'You can't go back to work for the king.'

Teg scoffs. 'Oh, don't worry about me. Those kitchens sapped the life out of me. I'll be happy never to wash another pan in my life. I think I'll take to the open road. I belong in the wilderness. Perhaps I'll find some other poor animals to fight for.'

At that, I smile. I don't know Teg very well, but I can tell he's not one for an ordinary life.

'Well, it looks like this is goodbye,' says Teg, and then he reaches down to tickle Cadno between the ears. 'You take care of your human now, won't you? There's a good boy. I promise he'll do the same for you.'

Cadno barks fondly, and Teg laughs before turning back to me.

'As soon as I'm out of sight, yes?'

I nod, and then Teg holds out his hand. I take it, and for a second we just stand there, not really shaking hands, but clasping them.

'Thank you, Charlie Challinor and friends,' he says. 'You have hearts of fire. Don't ever allow them to be extinguished.'

Without another word, Teg waves to us all and then slips through the ivy and out of sight.

'Cadno,' I say, unable to keep the tremor from my voice, and the cub steps forward as if he knows exactly what to do.

He stands before the curtain of ivy, and his fur takes on that familiar shimmer, dappling the walls with gold. His flames emerge in a mushroom of heat and light. Cadno swings his big, bushy tail round and, in one swipe, sets the gateway alight. I watch as the ivy goes up in flames, a brilliant waterfall of dazzling fire that blazes for what seems like an age. But then the ivy burns away into nothingness, and the fire disappears.

Where there was once a portal, there's now a wall of stone.

The gateway is gone. Forever.

Cadno is here to stay.

'Come on,' says Dad, putting his hand on my shoulder. 'Let's go home.'

'The first thing I'm doing is phoning your parents to let them know you're OK,' says Pa to Lippy and Roo. 'You're all still in big trouble, you know.'

Lippy and Roo groan as we make our way across the clearing. As we round the base of the north-west tower, Lippy pauses and lets out a gasp.

I turn. Everybody's frowning at her.

'Lippy, what's wrong?' I ask.

Lippy glances slowly up at the tower, as though she's slowly piecing things together. Then, finally, her face lights up.

'*To find the next pebble, you need to head north-west,*' she recites. 'That pebble you hid – it's up there, isn't it? Charlie! How were we ever supposed to get that?'

I shrug. 'I don't know what you're talking about.'

Lippy's lips narrow in determination. 'I'm going up there first thing tomorrow morning, and then I get to hide the next pebble, right?'

'Can't argue with the rules,' I say with a shrug.

Roo throws his head back and moans. 'Charlie, I told you to hide it somewhere she'd *never* find it!'

'Yeah, but if you think about it, if you hadn't told me to choose somewhere ridiculous, I wouldn't have hidden the pebble at the top of the tower. If I'd never hidden it at the top of the tower, I wouldn't have found the loose stones and used one to knock out the Grendilock. So technically, Roo, you saved us all!'

Roo ponders for a second and then starts to nod. 'Yeah . . . you're right. I'm a hero!'

'Just you guys wait,' Lippy says in a hushed, excited tone. 'I'm gonna hide it in the best place ever. You two will *never* find it.'

Roo and I smile at each other.

'With any luck,' I say under my breath, and together we walk into the night.

Chapter 25

The sky is still aglitter with stars when we get home.

Cadno is cuddled up against my chest. He looks dazed, like he's struggling to keep his eyes open. I don't blame him. After the last couple of days, I feel as though I could sleep for a week.

Lippy and Roo come home with us. Pa is true to his word – the first thing he does is ring their parents. Stella is enraged by Lippy's outing. Roo's dad didn't realize he was gone, and Pa assures him that he's fine and will be home in the morning.

'So was Tanya a monster that whole time?' Pa demands once the phone calls are out of the way. 'I dug out my best china teacups for her!'

We shuffle into the living room. Dad makes us all steaming mugs of hot chocolate. I take a sip, relishing the feeling of warmth spreading to the furthest reaches of my body.

'I've got a lot of explaining to do,' I say. Cadno is curled up on my lap, his belly rising and falling rhythmically. I realize then that this is the first time he's sat with me on the sofa. It feels natural. It feels *right*, like he belongs here with me.

Dad almost chokes on his hot chocolate. 'Understatement of the century!'

'And you'd better tell us *everything*, or I swear I will stop buying Coco Pops and make you eat muesli for breakfast,' says Pa.

The very prospect chills me to the bone. I glance at Lippy and Roo, who sit side by side on the sofa, silently nursing their mugs of hot chocolate as my dads and I talk.

I start at the beginning. I tell them the whole story – about Teg, Fargone, the Grendilock. I tell them everything that's happened over the last few weeks. By the time I'm done, Pa looks like he might be sick.

'Um, please say something.'

'The . . . the monster,' Pa stammers. 'Is it properly gone now?'

'Yes,' I say firmly. 'And the gateway is closed forever. Nothing can come through now.'

Pa glances from me to Cadno and back. 'And Cadno is . . . er, safe to be around?'

Cadno is fast asleep on my lap, making a little whistling snore with each breath.

'He's clearly an extremely deadly animal,' Dad grins. 'We should be very afraid.'

I laugh, and Pa blushes. 'I suppose we'd better buy him some toys, then, hadn't we?' he says.

I look up. Pa is smiling at me. Dad is smiling at him. Lippy and Roo are smiling at each other. We're all smiling and, for the first time in a long while, my heart feels full.

★

As much as Dad and Pa want to make up a bed for Cadno downstairs, I insist that he sleeps upstairs with me. It's what we're both used to. I don't think I could fall asleep without his warmth next to me now.

I kiss them both goodnight and retire to bed. I'm ready to challenge a sloth in the sleeping Olympics. Lippy and Roo have sleeping bags so that they can nest on my bedroom floor, and they promptly drift off to sleep. The excitement of the last few days is catching up with all of us.

I can hear my dads talking in the living room beneath me. Their voices are hushed, serious.

I suppose things will never really be the same again. It's not like we've got a regular pet or anything. We've got the last firefox. The last time I checked, there was no *Happy Firefox Handbook*.

Maybe I'll write it some day.

It'll take them a while to get used to it, to believe what is happening. Sometimes I still struggle with it myself. But they'll get there. I know they will.

They're my dads after all, and they're awesome.

I heave Cadno up so that I can rest my chin on his head. He grunts. I give him a kiss, right between his ears, and we fall asleep together. Two flames entwined.

Lippy and Roo are picked up early the next morning, and Cadno and I spend the next couple of days napping.

When we're not catching up on sleep, we're spending time downstairs with Dad and Pa. To my surprise, a day later I find a little doughnut-shaped doggie bed set up in the corner of the living room, along with a host of highly flammable-looking pet toys.

'Did you get all this?' I ask Pa.

Pa casts me a sheepish look. 'If he's staying, he might as well have nice things. I also bought some proper dog food, so you can stop feeding him corned beef.'

'I wondered where all of those packets disappeared to!' Dad exclaims. 'There wasn't enough for me to make my work sandwiches!'

I laugh and give each of them a hug, then watch as Cadno waddles over to a thick knot of colourful rope and prods it curiously with his nose. Within seconds, he's rampaging round the living room with the toy dangling from his jaws. I don't let him run around *too* much – the bite on his leg is still a bit swollen, but the anti-inflammatories that Stella gave him help a lot.

Dad also gets on the phone to the adoption agency, who unsurprisingly have never heard of Tanya Cleck. The receptionist won't tell him much, but, from what Dad can gather, Pam suffered an injury to the head and has no memory of the last few weeks, but should be OK in a few more. The receptionist apologizes and says we'll be receiving a home visit from another social worker soon.

'How do you feel about that, Charlie?' asks Pa.

'Good,' I say, and I realize I'm being sincere. I feel *really* good about it. The prospect of becoming a brother no longer fills me with fear and dread. 'Great, actually. I'm really excited!'

Dad and Pa beam.

'Us too,' says Dad, and then he gives my other dad a peck on the lips.

Some time later, there's a knock on the front door. Pa rushes to answer it, leaving me and Dad rolling a tennis ball across the floor, chuckling as Cadno scrambles after it.

I listen to the sound of Pa greeting whoever it is. Our guest has a familiar, booming voice. It starts to get closer – Pa has invited them inside. The living-room door opens, and Pa reappears.

'Charlie, there's somebody – well, several some-bodies, as a matter of fact – who would really like to see you,' he says, and he steps aside.

Standing there in the doorway are Stella, Lippy and Roo.

My heart feels like it's about to burst. The three of them give me a quick wave, but then their eyes go straight to Cadno.

'Hello, Charlie,' says Stella, leaning down next to him. Cadno doesn't object as she runs her hand from the top of his head all the way down to his bushy tail. 'How's the little one doing?'

'A lot better. The swelling has gone down now,' I say. 'Thank you for looking after him, Stella. You really saved him.'

Stella smiles. 'It was my pleasure, even if you did run off and nearly get yourselves killed.'

My cheeks burn, but Stella smiles.

'Is there anything else I can do for you?' she asks.

I shake my head. 'No, thank you. But you can call over to see him whenever you want, you know. Or we can bring him over to see you.'

Stella's laughter ricochets across the room. 'Oh, don't you worry. You won't be able to keep me away from this magnificent little creature!'

Cadno yaps happily.

'Don't make his head any bigger,' I say, laughing.

'We will actually be needing a fox-sitter soon,' Pa puts in. 'We can't exactly have a firefox wandering round the house when the new social worker comes to visit, can we?'

'It's a deal.' Stella grins. 'Well, I'll leave you all to it. I'm glad you're OK, Charlie, and that little Cadno is better. Lippy, I'll see you later.'

She gives us all a wave and exits the room. Lippy and Roo grin at me from the doorway.

'Dads?' I say.

Pa rolls his eyes. 'For goodness' sake, go. I can tell you're itching to escape from your embarrassing parents.'

Dad looks appalled. 'Speak for yourself! I'm a cool dad.'

'You're both cool dads,' I say, and then I scoop Cadno into my arms. 'I'll see you later.'

We shuffle out into the hallway, where Lippy and

Roo shower Cadno with strokes and kisses. This goes on for a while. When they're finally done, they seem to remember that I'm standing there, too.

'You all right, Charlie?' asks Roo.

'I'm all right, Roo. You?'

Roo nods.

'Lippy?'

Lippy puffs her cheeks out happily. 'I hid my pebble. I found yours at the top of the tower. You'll *never* find mine. Do you want to hear your clue?'

I laugh nervously. 'Er, yeah, but let's find somewhere to hang out first.'

'So where shall we go?' asks Roo.

'How about we go for a walk in the park?' I suggest. Cadno's ears perk up and his tongue lolls from his mouth. I think he's learned what the word 'walk' means.

When we get there, Cadno goes bounding over the grass, chasing after butterflies and sneezing when he gets too close to a fluffy dandelion clock.

'Can you believe that this is the same fearsome

creature that fought the Grendilock a few days ago?'
I laugh. Lippy and Roo both chuckle as Cadno
swipes at a dandelion spore that's stuck to his nose.

'Can *you* believe that you, *fearsome Charlie*, fought
the Grendilock a few days ago?' Lippy grins, shoving
me playfully on the shoulder.

'*Fearsome*,' I repeat. 'I've never been called that
before.'

My thoughts trail off as I catch the sound of two
unpleasantly familiar voices echoing through the
trees, accompanied by a rattling, clanging noise.

Will and Zack are at the skate park, dead ahead.

'Guys, maybe we should turn round?' I say. 'Let's
find somewhere a bit quieter, where Cadno can run –'

'Fancy seeing you here, goose food!'

Ugh, it's too late. I've been spotted.

Will leaps off the platform at the top of the tallest
ramp, his blond hair flopping over his forehead. Zack
follows him, his skateboard tucked under his arm.
They're both wearing slimy smirks on their faces,
which get even slimier when they see Cadno standing

by my feet. Behind them, a few other kids from school sit perched on top of the ramps.

'Hey,' says Will, nudging Zack with his elbow. 'Look, it's that fox again! Is he your best friend now, goose food? Have you finally given up on making real friends?'

I feel myself tense up. At my feet, Cadno begins to growl. Will laughs, and Zack joins in.

'Would you listen to him?' Will says, nodding at Cadno. 'He even *sounds* pathetic. No wonder you like him, goose food: you're both runts!'

He and his mate double over with laughter. My hands ball up into fists.

'Charlie . . .' says Lippy, grabbing my wrist. 'Come on, leave them to it.'

'And he was behind all that chaos at the fete, wasn't he?' Will goes on. 'You wait until I tell everybody that you and your freak pet caused the biggest disaster this town has seen in years!'

'I don't think you want to do that,' I say quietly.

Will freezes. He obviously hadn't expected me

to answer back. 'You what?'

'I said, I don't think you want to do that, Will,' I repeat. 'Or should I say . . . *Wilberforce, smoochums?*'

Will's face pales and Zack shoots him a horrified look.

'W-what did you just call me?' Will stammers.

'You heard,' I say. 'Or would you like me to say it a bit louder?'

I glance over Will's shoulder at our classmates, who are watching our exchange with interest. Will's eyes widen in alarm. Cadno snorts, like he's amused.

I look down at him, a seemingly ordinary fox cub. We might not be much to look at, but a few days ago we defeated a terrifying monster. And, if we can defeat the Grendilock, why would I still be scared of this pair of idiots?

'Now leave me alone, or I'll tell everybody what you're *really* called,' I say.

Will's gaze meets mine. 'You haven't got the guts,' he replies, but there's a tremor in his voice.

I smile. 'Haven't I?'

I see a glimmer of fear pass across his face.

'So,' I continue, 'get lost. And don't ever come after me or my friends again. Especially the four-legged one.'

Will's mouth narrows into a determined line. 'We're not scared of that little rat, are we, Zack?'

'Er, no,' Zack grunts uncertainly.

'Are you sure? Because he has a very . . . *fiery* temper.'

Cadno lets out a ferocious bark as if to emphasize my point. Zack gulps. 'Will, maybe we should go . . .'

'Yes, I think you should,' I agree. 'Cadno is getting twitchy.'

Cadno takes a single step forward, and Will and Zack both stumble backwards in fright.

'We were going anyway,' says Will hastily, and, just as they turn, I lean down and pat Cadno on the back.

'Get 'em, boy!'

Cadno races forward, barking furiously. Will and Zack each let out a strangled scream and run for it. Will, in his panic, hops on to his skateboard – but it goes flying out from under him, sending him sprawling into a bush.

Cadno stops, glances at him pityingly, and then wees on the bush. Zack, meanwhile, has completely vanished. Our classmates howl with laughter.

'Nice one, Charlie!'

'Your fox is so *cute*! Where did you get him?'

I grin and don't spare Will another glance as I march off down the path. Lippy and Roo rush to catch up with me.

'That was amazing!' Lippy exclaims. 'Did you see their faces?'

'Wilberforce,' says Roo. 'Is his name actually Wilberforce?'

'Oh yes, if his mum's lunchtime phone calls are anything to go by!'

Lippy roars with laughter. 'That is absolutely brilliant. I don't think he's going to bother you any more, Charlie.'

I laugh, too, because I know she's right.

'But everybody's seen Cadno now,' Roo points out.

'That doesn't matter,' I say. 'I don't need to hide him any more. He's part of the family now, and I'm proud of him. And with the Grendilock gone he's got no reason to be scared or angry, so I think we'll be seeing a lot less of his fiery side.'

Cadno races round us in joyful circles as we carry on with our walk through the park. The sun is shining and, while summer is only visiting, Cadno's here to stay. Together, we can take on the whole world – as long as we steer clear of geese, that is.

Acknowledgements

My first thanks go to Amber Caravéo, super-agent extraordinaire. You have helped me learn the essentials of story, and I will forever be in your debt for all of the wisdom and encouragement. I think we did all right, didn't we? Look, Cadno found a home with Puffin!

Which brings me on to my second thanks – to my lovely editor, Ben Horslen. Thank you so much for all of your editorial expertise and for making my journey as a debut author so dreamy!

To Shreeta Shah, Wendy Shakespeare, Sean Williams, Ken de Silva, Jill Tytherleigh, Phoebe Williams, Evelyn Opoku-Agyeman, Alice Grigg, Beth Fennell and the Rights crew, and everybody else in the Puffin team who has worked on this book – thank you from the bottom of my heart!

I always dreamed of having an illustrated book, and Laura Catalán truly brought Cadno and his friends and enemies to life in a way I could never have imagined. Thank you for your magic!

To the people who read this story in its early stages: Anna Britton, you helped to shape the opening chapters of this book; Lesley Parr, you have been my closest companion on this journey, and I always find joy in our friendship (and those moments when your cat flashes her bottom at me when we're Skyping).

To everybody in the Team Skylark WhatsApp group: you're all bonkers, but in the best possible way. I do mention goats in Chapter 10 – does that count? If not, here goes: goatgoatgoatgoat. Thank you all for cheering me on!

To all the friends I've met through Twitter and Instagram: Mia Kuzniar, Benjamin Dean, Rosie Talbot, George Lester and so many others. I've turned to you all at various points throughout this journey to publication, and I hope I get to meet you all in person someday.

And, lastly, thank you to my family. To my mother, for listening to my updates and never faltering in your belief in me, to my brother and sister for your endless support, to my mother-in-law for being an amazing cheerleader, and to my Nan and Grampa for taking me to bookshops when I was but a little firefox cub. You're all lush.

And proper lastly this time, I promise, thank you to Tom and Parker. You fill my life with love and light and happiness. I hope I've made you both proud.